DREAMERS

DREAMERS

A Dream-Catchers Novel

SHAWN DALTON-SMITH

Indulge a Dream Publishing LLC

Cover Artist: Taria Reed

Dedication

This work is dedicated to my loving and supportive husband. Thank you, sweetie. You believed in me when I didn't believe in myself. The only reason I can write an epic romance is because I am part of one. You will always be my ride-or-die.

To Ashley: My eldest child and daughter, who read every word (even though some of them caused a blush or two) and gave me constructive criticism. And who always got my weird sense of humor.

To Janay: My middle child. You were always able to make me laugh, even when I felt like crying. You may not know it, but you are still able to do that for me.

To Alex: My youngest child, and only son. Always able to appreciate the creative process. It seems we have that in common. Keep that creativity alive, son.

For all my children: Don't let anyone kill your dreams. Dream on!

Chapter 1

Somiar stole a peek at herself in the mirror. The long black hair and tiger-like eyes that weren't her own no longer bothered her. The first time she'd seen another face staring back at her in a mirror scared her so badly, she woke up in a cold sweat. Learning to enjoy it took some doing.

Ah, the perks of a dream. She could do as she pleased, be whoever she wanted to be, say whatever she wanted to say, without consequence. Anything was possible.

The mystery was still unsolved about why her subconscious bought her back to the Lunar Hotel night club several times a month. She'd been here once, during a bachelorette party for an old college friend, Kalyste.

Kalyste was hit by a car that night. The worst part was her maid of honor was the driver. Although she and Kalyste had been close in college, they'd drifted apart after graduation. It had been well over a year since that horrible night. The strange dreams started about six months ago.

Something was different about tonight. A strange energy filled the air. Her senses were on high alert. An invisible force pulled at her, but she didn't know from where, or to what.

What is she doing here?

Somiar jumped. She turned, expecting to find someone standing behind her, but no one was there.

2

Where is the necklace?

There it was again. A woman's voice. But there wasn't a woman within ten feet. Oh, wow. She was really letting her dreams get to her. Now she was hearing disembodied voices. What was that all about?

Somiar decided to let the dream take over. Maybe if she stopped controlling everything, she would find her answer. Her foot tapped to the beat of the loud, throbbing, hip-hop music. Nothing would be better than to toss her inhibitions and join the crowd on the dance floor. Leaning against the mirrored wall, she scanned the dim room to choose a partner. Her gaze settled on a man in the corner with dark chocolate skin and short coal-black hair. He was sitting at a corner table and from this distance, with the lights so dim, he seemed good-looking. But she had seen way too many men in clubs who appeared attractive until the lights came on.

Attempting to gain a better look at him, she moved in closer. His dark blue polo shirt fit just right across his broad chest. Big, muscular arms rested on the wooden table, one hand toying with the straw in his empty glass. He seemed content to survey the crowd while his friend talked to an attractive woman. Strange, but Somiar got the feeling the woman was watching her. A chill ran down her spine, and she tore her gaze away, turning her attention back to the man she had set her sights on.

This might be interesting. She flashed him a smile when he glanced her way. Her pulse quickened in anticipation. C'mon Daddy, let Mamma see that smile. She winked at him as she sipped her drink, pleased to see straight white teeth beneath full lips when he smiled back.

Always a sucker for a handsome smile, Somiar sauntered over and placed her drink on his table, then leaned toward him, so he could get a good view of her cleavage. His gaze slid up and down her body, peeling her clothes away one layer at a time.

She returned his bold survey, eyebrows rising in appreciation and panties moistening at the sight of the bulge in his pants. Lord, don't wake me now. "Care to dance, handsome?"

"How could I refuse?" Her body vibrated at the deep, sexy, almost hypnotic sound of his voice. He stood at least six inches taller than Somiar, and was all muscle. Damn. Where were all the men like him when she was awake? She glided ahead of him onto the packed dance space.

The fog, generated from a machine in the ceiling, and the dim lights added just the right sexy ambiance. Crowded dancing bodies flashed in and out of her vision with the flashing lights. She pressed her back up against his chest on the dance floor, her hips gyrating against him, the heat from him intense. The masculine smell of his body surrounded her, sweat mixed with the spicy scent of his cologne. His erection against the top of her ass excited her.

When his movement suddenly stilled, she turned to face him, and looped her arm around his waist.

Looking up at his face, she noticed he seemed to have lost interest in her. His gaze went from person to person as if looking for someone. She wasn't used to being ignored and his preoccupation irritated the hell out of her. Putting a hand to his cheek, she regained his attention. "Something wrong, handsome?"

He stepped back from her and his eyes narrowed. "You tell me."

She didn't like his tone. There was a strange light coming from his right hand. The glowing red ring on his finger made her shudder. It was almost... sinister. "It's just a dream." She whispered the words and let them play over and over in her head.

The music ended, and Somiar left the dance floor without a backward glance. The hairs on the back of her neck stood up. She knew he was following her. Was he some kind of stalker? Okay, now she was really losing it. A dream stalker? She paused at the edge of the dance floor, hoping it was just her overactive imagination, and he would keep walking. He stood so close, she felt his body heat on her back.

"What are you?" His voice was hostile.

Somiar turned, eyes wide. "What did you say?"

He grabbed her wrist so tightly, her pulse throbbed in her thumb. She couldn't take her eyes off the glowing red ring on his finger. "I said what are you?"

"What're you doing? Are you crazy? Let go of me." Several people turned to stare as she desperately tried to free herself from his grasp. She squeezed her eyes shut, expecting to wake up in her comfortable bedroom. Something was wrong. Why couldn't she wake up? Her heart pounded and a bead of sweat trickled down her face. Blind panic threatened to overtake her when she realized she was trapped in her dream. There had to be a way out.

His grip tightened. The lips she found so tempting just moments ago stretched to a nasty grin. "Oh, I don't think so."

"Malachi, over here!"

His head turned toward the deep masculine voice from across the room.

Somiar drove her knee into his groin, and he loosened his grip. Without looking back, she ran for the exit. Taking the stairs as fast as she could, a familiar dizziness overwhelmed her. She was falling, and grateful the dream was about to be over.

Her body jerked at the sound of the alarm clock clanging next to her. She slammed her hand on the off button and listened to the familiar hum of the ceiling fan while she attempted to slow her heartbeat. What happened? Maybe giving up control wasn't such a good idea after all. Apparently, getting it back wasn't an easy task.

Her late night out with her friends was something she had been looking forward to for weeks. With their busy lives, it was hard to find time for each other. That was why she chose to catch a couple of winks before they hit the Atlanta scene. She never knew what time they would be getting in. One thing was certain. The Lunar Hotel nightclub would not be one of their stops.

She dragged herself out of bed and into her bathroom to start the shower. She reached for the knob and stared in confusion at the faint bruise on her wrist.

***

Malachi lay on the floor holding his crotch, praying for the pain to subside. Stephen stood over him and held out his hand to help his partner up.

Ignoring him, Malachi struggled to his feet, "Go after her." He could barely choke the words out. "She's a Dreamer. Go after her."

"Get it together. People are staring at you. In my office.

Now." Stephen stalked off across the crowded club and down a hall behind the bar.

Unable to figure out Stephen's attitude, Malachi followed, eyes tearing. "I know a Dreamer when I see one."

"You went after the wrong woman. She had no idea what was going on." Stephen continued down the hall at a brisk pace, never bothering to see if Malachi followed. "Listen to me. We were supposed to be concentrating on one thing and one thing only. Keeping Lucien safe." He threw his arms in the air in exasperation. "It's not rocket science. Did she give you any indication that she was after him?"

Malachi struggled to keep up. His dick still hurt like hell, and he had a feeling Stephen was walking fast on purpose. "No. But she was a Dreamer and that can't mean anything good." Malachi remembered lessons from his training days. The only good Dreamer was a dead one. Or at the very least, one that was out of commission.

"Listen Mal, maybe she was a Dreamer, but she wasn't after Lucien. Besides, if she was our girl, she would have tried to kill you, not dance with you. There's always one Dreamer for one mark, and I have my Dreamer out of commission in the back. I already gave The Keepers the location of her body."

As much as he would have liked to argue the point, he couldn't. Stephen was right. They had caught a young Dreamer once, out on her first assignment, and she sang like a canary. Dreamers never worked in pairs. They all shared a connection. A connection that only served as a distraction. Since they were trying to keep their existence a secret, and avoid being caught by the Catchers, distractions could prove disastrous.

Malachi followed Stephen into the back office and shut the door, blocking the noise from outside. He stared at the woman lying on the couch, eyes closed, in a deep sleep. Her coffee complexion was flawless, her face, relaxed. Light brown curls spilled over the sofa cushions. The white silk mini-dress didn't leave much to the imagination. Her breasts almost fell out of the plunging neckline. Her tapered waist led to softly curving hips. "What a waste of a perfect body."

Stephen pulled out his ringing cell phone and rolled his eyes. "Get real. That's a figment of her imagination. Who knows what she really looks like?" He tapped a button on the phone and raised it to his ear. "Is the body there? Good, we're ready on this end." Both men watched in silence as the unconscious woman slowly faded, leaving the star-shaped, metal pronged pin behind.

Shaking his head, Malachi walked away from the couch. "How'd you know she was after Lucien?" Stephen had been a Catcher for almost twenty years. He didn't make careless mistakes. Malachi had been doing it for seven and was still considered wet behind the ears.

"She said if I didn't do as I was told, Lucien was a dead man. I got her before she got me or Lucien, no thanks to you."

Malachi turned back to Stephen. "What do you mean no thanks to me? Do you honestly think I would have intentionally left you alone with a Dreamer? I'm telling you the other one could have just as easily been after Lucien." If anything had happened to Stephen, Malachi knew he would never forgive himself. Stephen was more than a partner; he was like an older brother.

Malachi ran his hands over his face. "Look man, I'm sorry.

I fucked up. But you know I got your back and you got mine. Right?" Malachi held his fist out.

Stephen smiled and gave Malachi a fist tap. "No doubt."

"How's Lucien anyway?"

"He's safe. He was so hammered, I don't think he knew anything was going on. Anyway, the Keepers want us to talk to him. They think it's time he is told about his destiny."

Malachi sat on the corner of the desk sighing heavily. "You know this isn't going to go well. It never does." He remembered the way he'd freaked out when Stephen told him about being a Dream-Catcher. It had taken him months to listen. Until a Dreamer tried to decapitate him.

"Yeah, I know." Stephen crossed the room and gazed at the camera surveillance of the hotel club, worry marring his features. The silver strands in his hair glinted in the light.

Malachi got the hint. Stephen always acted preoccupied when he didn't want to discuss something. Truth was, Malachi didn't want to think about how Lucien would react either. If only the boy's father were still alive. It would have been so much easier if Richard were there to prepare him for his new life. Thanks to the Dreamers, Lucien would never know what a phenomenal man his father was.

Malachi decided to change the subject. "You never did tell me how you got the Dreamer pinned. Care to share the story?"

Stephen retrieved his pin from the white leather couch. "You caused quite a stir grabbing that girl. It distracted the Dreamer long enough for me to grab hold of the gun she had jammed in my side and pin her. I told security that my date had too much to drink, and I was going to let her sleep it off in the back. Who's going to argue with the boss? Then I called you."

Malachi stood, and set to pacing the floor. "You got the drop on her because I grabbed a girl? Don't you think it was strange that you were able to catch her so easily? You and Lucien should have been dead. What happened?"

"I don't know, Mal. It's been bugging the hell out of me too. Maybe your girl was a Dreamer and my girl sensed her." Stephen poured a shot of tequila and downed it in one gulp. "Strange though. The two of them shouldn't have been in the same place, even if they had separate marks. They don't usually make mistakes like that. But we got our girl, so let's drop it and report to the Dream Keepers for our next assignment."

Chapter 2

Somiar stifled a yawn and rolled her eyes. Good grief, does he ever shut up? She saw his lips moving but all she heard was blah, blah, blah.

Dr. Michael Morgan had caught her attention a month ago when he moved into her building. He had a sexy smile and a great body. His skin was the color of peanut butter with not a blemish on it. But it was his eyes that drew a woman in. Sea green eyes, that sparkled every time he smiled. Somiar suspected they were contacts but never asked. There was an air of confidence about him that intrigued her.

She had begun arranging chance meetings. They'd bumped into each other several times on the elevator, and jogged at the same time on the trail in the park across the street. When he asked her out for lunch, she accepted.

At first, she attributed his non-stop talking to first-date nerves. Now, on their second date, she wanted to duct tape his mouth shut.

The snow-white linen and sterling silver on the table was spotless. Silver bowls filled with fresh white roses adorned the dessert table holding a magnificent chocolate fountain surrounded by large strawberries and assorted pastries. The jazz band in the corner of the room was outstanding, playing softly while a few couples danced close on the small dance floor.

Her fingers toyed with the stem of her crystal water glass. Were she with someone who didn't bore her to tears, she would have found the evening romantic. Eyeing the other patrons in the restaurant, Somiar tried to think of a good excuse to end the night early.

She did a double take when she spotted the man from her dream in the corner. It can't be. She slid her index finger under her diamond bracelet and rubbed the slightly tender bruise on her wrist.

"What are you?" His words replayed in her mind. When he turned his head to look at her, the hairs on the back of her neck stood up, and she inhaled sharply. She didn't realize she was staring until he smiled and raised his glass in a mock salute.

She dragged her gaze back to her dinner companion. He still hadn't stopped talking. "I still remember the first time I did a colonoscopy." Blah, blah, blah.

When her cell phone rang, she jerked it out of her purse, grateful for the interruption. She glanced at the display window. A small picture of her mother illuminated screen. "Excuse me, Michael, I have to take this." As she stood and headed for the ladies' room, she pushed the talk button on her phone. "Hello, Monica. You don't know how glad I am to hear from you. This man is driving me nuts."

Somiar sat on one of the plush chairs in front of a mirror and checked her make up. Her light brown skin was flawless, but her brown spiral curls had started to droop. Just like my date, she sighed to herself, pushing a curl behind her ear.

"Listen to me, Somiar, I need to see you. We have to talk. Can you come by tonight?"

She frowned. Whenever her mother wanted to see her, it usually spelled trouble. Once, she had called Somiar because she needed someone to take the dorky son of a business partner out for a night on the town. That man made Michael look like Prince Charming. He spent the whole night complaining about his allergies. He swore he was allergic to everything.

But Monica's interruption provided a perfect out from this date. "This is really short notice, but it gives me a good excuse to ditch blabber mouth. What I really want to do is go home to my comfortable, warm bed."

"No! You can't go to sleep. You have to come see me first." There was an unsettling urgency in Monica's voice.

Somiar's heart did a little flip. "Is everything okay? Are you all right? What's happened?"

"Don't get upset. Nobody's hurt, but I need to talk to you tonight. Promise you'll come right over."

Somiar wanted to ask more questions but decided against it. If there was bad news, she didn't want to hear it in the middle of the ladies' room. "I'll be right there. I just have to say goodbye to my date. I'll see you in about half an hour."

Shoving her phone back in her purse, she hurried out the bathroom door into the hall and ran face-first into a broad chest. Crying out, she dropped the purse. "Excuse me. I didn't see you standing..." Her words trailed off as she looked up into her dream man's hazel eyes. Her stomach fluttered and her heart pounded.

"It's all right. No harm done." He gestured at her scattered items on the floor. May I?"

A heated rush ran through her body at the sound of his voice. "Yes, thank you." She took a deep breath and fought for composure, despite not being able to take her eyes off his ass when he bent to retrieve the contents of her purse. When he straightened, and returned her purse, she gave him a timid smile. "Have we met? You look familiar." Somiar silently prayed he would say no. Last night was only a dream. It had to be. She was being silly. But still. Here he was, in the flesh.

"I don't think so. I'm Malachi Walker, and you are?"

She stared dumbly at his extended hand, and fought back the panic bubbling up in her chest. Malachi. It is him. How can this be? "Somiar. My name is Somiar. Somiar Ayers."

Malachi withdrew his hand, and gestured at the men's room door behind her. "If you'll excuse me, Ms. Ayers."

"Oh, yes. Of course." Leave now. You sound like an idiot. She was rooted to the spot and willed her feet to move. Okay, I must have seen him somewhere before, then dreamed about him.

When he disappeared behind the bathroom door, she hurried back to her table. "Michael, I have to go. Family emergency." She didn't give him a chance to respond and practically ran from the dining room to her car and peeled out of the parking lot.

***

Somiar hugged the housekeeper who opened the door to her mother's opulent home.

"Somiar, how nice to see you. Ms. Ayers is in her study. She's been waiting for you."

"Thanks, Tessa. Is everything okay? She sounded upset on the phone, but she wouldn't say what was going on." Somiar looked for any sign in Tessa's plump face that there was some catastrophe.

"All I know is she got a phone call about two hours ago, and she's been shut up in there ever since. I'll tell her you're here."

"No, Tessa. You go on to bed, it's late and I don't feel like driving home, so I'll spend the night here in my old bed-room." She smiled as the elderly lady briskly left the room. She couldn't recall a time when Tessa ever slowed down.

Somiar ran her hand over the cool marble banister as she went up the wide staircase. Stopping at the first landing, she turned left and twisted the brass knob on the mahogany dou-ble doors.

When it opened, she frowned at the sight of her mother sitting on the red suede couch, staring at the empty fireplace, a brandy glass clutched in her palms. Somiar rarely saw her mother even have a glass of wine and had never seen her drink hard liquor. She always said limited alcohol helped her stay pretty. At sixty-five, Monica Ayers was still a beautiful woman. Her mocha skin was smooth and wrinkle free save the small lines in the corners of her eyes. Her long, shiny, silver hair was pulled back in a French twist.

The thick, white carpet muffled Somiar's steps. She had al-ways loved this room. It was so quiet and cozy. Her mother called it her sanctuary. It hadn't changed much. The book-cases lining one wall still held the same rare books. The large mahogany desk always boasted a white vase full of black dyed roses, with one white rose in the center of the bouquet. When she was little, Somiar had asked about the strange arrangement, but Monica had just shrugged. "I happen to like black roses."

"Monica? What's going on?" Somiar sat down and placed a gentle hand on her mother's shoulder.

Monica looked over at her then quickly turned away. Her eyes were vacant. Nothing in her face gave even a hint of what to expect. "Oh," she said "I'm glad you're here. I was afraid you might not come." She took a small sip of brandy from her glass. "Now that you're here, I don't know where to start."

Somiar gave her a nervous smile. "Okay, you're really freaking me out. Just tell me what's wrong." Monica was always the picture of composure. She never beat around the bush or was at a loss for words. Somiar envied her mother's ability to rein in her emotions. No one ever caught her off guard. She always seemed to have the upper hand. Although it kept them from being as close as a mother and daughter should be, it seemed to make Monica's life easier.

But it made things harder for Somiar. When she started preschool, she discovered it wasn't normal for a mother to insist that her daughter call her by her first name. Monica would never give Somiar a reason. "Just do as I ask," was all she would say. Her mother also thought public displays of affection were disgusting. But she wasn't very affectionate in private either. Many times, Somiar wondered what it would take to make her mother love her. As she got older, she accepted her mother's stand-offish attitude as a fact of life. Seeing her so frazzled tonight was unnerving.

"What I have to tell you will be hard to believe. No matter how strange it sounds, you must not interrupt me until I'm finished." Monica sounded as though she had to force the words out.

"I promise." Somiar folded her hands in her lap and tried to brace herself for the coming bad news.

Monica rose and stood next to the massive fireplace. Her fingers traced the silver framed picture of herself taken when she was about Somiar's age. "Twenty-five years ago, I was part of a group called Dreamers. We all have special gifts that we learned to control. When we go to sleep at night, we can go anywhere we wanted and do what we wanted."

Somiar's head jerked up. Those few sentences sounded far too familiar. Gooseflesh rose on her arms.

"We can even change our appearance." There was a faraway look in Monica's eyes. "We can interact with the people. They could see us, talk with us, touch us, and never know our actual bodies were somewhere else in a deep sleep. We got away with pretty much anything because the laws of nature didn't apply to us. In the dream state, we don't leave fingerprints or DNA."

"You're not making any sense. Are you trying to tell me you can astral-project? It's not possible." Somiar's heart pounded. Her fingers dug into the soft padding of the couch. This couldn't be happening. If this was true, it would explain her dream last night. But why would Monica withhold such information from her?

"If you would just listen to me, I can explain. People who claim to astral-project supposedly do it through meditation and travel to another plane of existence. We have to sleep, and we stay right here on this plane, in this time." Monica drained her glass.

Somiar remembered her dream. It was a dream, wasn't it?

She leaned forward, elbows on knees and rested her forehead in her palms. "It can't be."

"The Dreamers work for a group called the Legacy. The group hires Dreamers as trained assassins to eliminate rid of anyone who might be a threat to other Dreamers or, if the price is right, anyone else. The biggest thorn in our side is another group called Dream Keepers. They have their own trained men, the Dream Catchers. A Dream Catcher's job is to stop Dreamers from making the hit." Monica kept talking as if Somiar had never spoken.

The question of her dream man echoed in her head. *What are you?*

"Assassins? You're talking about murder. I've heard enough." Somiar shook her head and started towards the door. "If this is your idea of a joke, it's not funny." Part of her was sure Monica wasn't kidding, and she felt the need to run out of there. "You know what? I don't even want to know." If she was projecting at night, then fine. But no way was she going to be part of some cloak-and-dagger assassins' club. She opened the door, only to have Monica slam it shut again.

Monica stood between her and the door, a wild look in her eyes. "Somiar, you're a Dreamer. You're a Dreamer and I'm not your mother."

The words came from Monica in such a rush, it took a moment for Somiar to process them. "What did you say?"

"You're a Dreamer." Monica walked away, keeping her back to Somiar.

"That's not what I'm talking about and you know it."

"I'm not your mother."

"Turn around and look at me, Monica." Somiar put a firm

hand on Monica's shoulder, wanting to see her eyes when she said the words. "Look at me and repeat what you just said."

Monica turned and faced her. Their gazes locked, and without batting a lash she repeated her words. "I'm not your mother."

"Is this why you raised me the way you did? Why did you even take me if you knew you would never accept me as your own? Why bother?" Somiar flopped down on the couch, letting her head rest against the back.

"You seem more at odds with the fact that you're adopted than the fact that you're a Dreamer. Monica gave her a small glass of brandy. "Here, drink this." She sat next to Somiar and put her hand on her knee. "So, you knew."

"I didn't know anything. I thought I was having dreams. Dreams I could control." She drained her glass in one gulp, wincing as it burned its way down her throat. "I've been dealing with weird dreams for years. I'm just relieved to hear I'm not alone. That there's an explanation." Somiar turned her head to the side. "Who's my real mother? Did you know her?" Before Monica could answer, Somiar pressed on. "Can she do this dreamer thing too?"

"One thing at time." Monica took the glass from her and brushed her hair back. Her voice soft, soothing. And totally out of character for Monica. "Your mother and I were Dreamers and best friends. Although there was a twenty-year age difference, our mutual gift provided a special bond between us. Dreamers always recognize each other, even when our appearance is changed. We are all connected. That's why there's always one Dreamer for one mark unless the Dreamer is in training."

Somiar yawned and fought to keep her eyes open. "I feel funny. What did you do to me?"

Monica lifted Somiar's legs from under her and laid them on the couch. "Just relax, Somiar. I didn't want you to have any doubts about what I'm about to tell you. Just lie back and let go. Close your eyes and think about me, this house, and this room. Drift."

Somiar let the weight of her eyelids take over. A familiar weightlessness descended on her, followed by a moment of darkness. When she opened her eyes, she was standing behind the potted palm in the corner of her mother's study.

Monica had resumed her position in front of the fireplace. "We always materialize and return to our bodies out of public view. I've been told it's an inborn survival instinct."

Somiar stepped from behind the plant and glanced around the room. She walked toward Monica and stopped dead in her tracks when she saw her own body lying on the couch. Her mouth went dry and her tongue felt thick. Sweat beaded on her forehead.

Monica approached her with a glass of water. "Here. I promise nothing's in it. You'll be able to taste the water. If it were alcohol, it would have no effect on you. You can't get drunk in a dream state."

"What did you give me? Am I hallucinating?" Somiar took the glass with shaking hands, unable to take her eyes off her sleeping body.

Monica smiled at her. "I gave you something to make you sleep. Don't worry. It was a minute dose. The effect will only last for about an hour. It's something I kept after I stopped working for the Legacy."

Her face heated at the group's name. "How could you be a cold-blooded killer? You've never been big on affection, but murder? Where is my mother and why did she give me up? Where's my father?" The composure in her voice scared her. There were no hysterics. Only a frightening calm.

Monica held up one hand, her smile fading. She pressed her fingers against her temples and inhaled. "As a Dreamer, you'll find there are people who want you out of commission whether you work for the Legacy or not. Those people view us as a threat, and in all fairness, some of us are. Dreamers know they can get away with just about anything, and some of them did everything. Rape, robbery, murder."

Somiar remembered her own thoughts from the night before. Be whoever, say whatever, do whatever, all without consequence. It was euphoric. No doubt, she had been tempted on more than one occasion to cross certain taboo boundaries. How many times had she been dreaming and seen a piece of jewelry she wanted? Or wanted to annihilate someone who pissed her off? She hadn't known her actions were real. Hadn't realized there were consequences.

Luckily, her personal beliefs wouldn't let her cross the line. It wasn't her nature to take something that wasn't hers or end a life. Thank heaven she had never done anything to hurt anyone.

"They interfered in the lives of others regardless of who got hurt. That's why the Dream Catchers organized. The problem was, the Dream Catchers wanted all Dreamers neutralized. They left us no choice. It became a matter of survival. We needed money to stay alive and that's why we became paid assassins." Monica waved her arms around the room. "Very well-paid assassins."

Somiar ignored the bile rising in her throat and inhaled deeply. "Oh, and murder for money is so much more honorable." How could Monica condemn murder one minute and condone it the next? She was one big contradiction.

"The people who are marked by The Legacy are slime. They are the rapist, pedophiles, and scum of society. Quite a few of them got away with it because they're in a position of power. Untouchable. Once someone petitions The Legacy and the money is paid, the job is done."

Somiar could only stare at her in fascination. The woman who raised her was standing there trying to justify murder. What was worse, she believed the crap she was spewing.

"Every once in a while, we do a little pro bono work. Usually, we had something to do with those karma stories you hear on the news." Monica seemed pleased with herself. "Come on Somiar, you know what I'm talking about. Some man rapes and kills a little girl from a poor family but gets away with it because the police mangle the investigation. Suddenly, he does something stupid like shoots himself in the face with his own gun while cleaning it."

Monica rolled her eyes heavenward. "Really? Of course, the police aren't going to dig too deep into his death. They're more than eager to write it off as an accident. They don't like the scum bastards any more than we do. That makes it easier on us."

"What gives you the right to play God?" Somiar knew right then and there, she may be a Dreamer, but the Legacy could go to hell. They sounded like a bunch of vigilante lunatics.

What pissed her off even more was the fact that she had been lied to her whole life. She wanted answers. And Monica could provide them. "My life has been a lie. I take it your late husband isn't my father. Who is?"

Monica nibbled on her lower lip. "You might want to sit down for this." When she didn't, Monica took a deep breath. "I was never married. I thought a dead father would be a lot easier to take than knowing your mother got pregnant during a one -night stand."

On rubber legs, Somiar made her way to an overstuffed chair and collapsed on the cushions. "How could you? How could you do that? What in your brain made you think that was a good decision?"

"Don't get sassy with me. I did what I thought was right." Monica assumed her no-nonsense tone, the one she used whenever she thought Somiar was out of line.

Somiar seethed. Maybe Monica wasn't her real mother, but after all these years, that tone still worked. Her gaze strayed back to her sleeping form on the couch. "You told me you inherited your money and the business from your mother."

"I did. We had to have a valid record of income, and a way to keep the money I made from the Legacy clean." Monica crossed the room and lit a cigarette. "The Legacy made arrangements for her to buy islands and resorts all over the world. Having members of the Legacy in key government roles made acquiring land easy."

Somiar gasped. "Keep your money clean? You mean you're using the resorts to launder your money." She didn't need Monica to confirm her accusation. The deafening silence was all the answer she needed. She took a few deep breaths trying to make sense of everything. Is my mother dead? Why did you raise me?"

"Your mother, Leila, was twenty years old when she had you. Dreamers can only have one child, and they are always girls. Those girls are always Dreamers, and they are expected to be trained by their mothers to work for The Legacy." Monica took a long drag from her cigarette then crossed the room to her desk. She sat back in the plush leather chair and flicked her ash. "Leila didn't want that life for you, so when she found out I was retiring, she asked me to adopt you. We kept her pregnancy a secret, and you were legally adopted by me after you were born. Although you were to be told that you were a Dreamer, I was not supposed to train you for the Legacy. As far as they know, I adopted a normal female child."

"Then they don't know about me. They never even suspected?" Somiar found that just a little hard to believe.

"Of course, there was always a chance that the Legacy would find out about you. That's why I took it upon myself to make sure you took self-defense classes. If they knew, they might have come after you." Monica smashed her cigarette in the marble ashtray.

"You were supposed to tell me I was a Dreamer. Why didn't you?"

"I just did."

There was no point in trying to argue with Monica. Somiar had learned a long time ago that Monica did what Monica wanted to do. To hell with anybody who didn't agree. "You said my real mother's name is Leila. Is she still alive? Where is she?"

Monica's lips quivered. "Your mother is why you're here tonight. While on assignment last night at a party in the Lunar Hotel ballroom, there was a hitch she wasn't prepared for. Her mark was a future Dream Catcher. There were two trained Catchers guarding him, but she was prepared for that. She was about to eliminate one of them when she saw the other one grab you. I was there watching from the other end of the room. I wasn't supposed to be there." Monica gave Somiar a look that riveted her to the floor. "You weren't supposed to be there either. I've been watching her for years. Even though I retired, I still worried about her, but there was nothing I could do. She's now being held by The Dream Keepers, and you have to get her back."

***

Malachi sat at his private table in one of the hotel restaurants staring into his glass. He couldn't get Somiar out of his mind. From the moment he saw her, he was intrigued. Those penetrating eyes of hers held an invitation. At least, that's what he'd hoped when he followed her to the bathroom. After she stared him down and then left the table, he'd thought it was an invitation. He'd never felt more foolish in his life when he realized meeting him in the back wasn't her intention. She'd looked at him like he'd lost his mind when he introduced himself. Her seductive voice and skin the color of simmering brown sugar kept invading his brain. There was also something familiar about her. He couldn't quite put his finger on it, but something about her tugged at his memory.

Stephen slid into the booth across from Malachi. "Sorry I'm late. I had a little trouble convincing Lucien to meet us.

He's still celebrating his birthday. The Watchers are having a hell of a time keeping up with him."

"Well, he's twenty-one and just inherited a ton of money. After tonight, his life is going to change. I say let him have his fun while he can." Malachi drained his glass.

"What's got you in such a mood?" Stephen stretched his legs out.

"Nothing. Just one of those days. Lucien's a good guy. He'll be fine." Malachi inclined his head toward the entrance. "Speak of the devil."

Stephen and Malachi watched as Lucien strode across the room. Numerous women turned to watch his progress. At six three, with a cocky, self-assured air about him, Lucien always attracted female attention.

Stephen moved over next to Malachi and motioned for Lucien to sit.

"Alright guys, where's the fire?" Lucien sat back in his chair and drummed his fingers on the table. "Can we make this quick? I'm supposed to meet someone in a few minutes"

"Looks like you're going to have to cancel." Stephen slid his phone over to Lucien. "Now."

Lucien knew not to push Stephen too far. Pulling his own phone from his pocket, he tapped the screen with his thumbs, then returned the phone to its place. "I know you and my father were friends, but can you stop the watching over me bullshit? I'm a big boy now and it's pissing me off."

"Your father and your inheritance are the reason we need to talk to you." Stephen motioned to the waitress.

"If you're worried about my inheriting Dad's partnership in the hotel chain, don't. I don't plan to step on any toes, and since the will prevents me from selling unless it's to either of you, there's no issue." Lucien ordered a drink from the waitress and gave her an appreciative smile. She smiled back at him, an exaggerated wiggle in her hips when she walked away.

Malachi sat back and rolled his eyes. "Lucien, pay attention. You're a fool if you plan to own part of a business and not get involved in how it's run. But your part in the hotel is not what we're interested in."

Lucien looked baffled. "It can't be the money. You two have more money than you could ever spend in your lifetime, or am I wrong?"

"No, you're not wrong. What we're interested in is a ring your father left you. One that looks like this." Stephen stretched his arm across the table, showing off the platinum ring with the large black stone in the middle.

"You guys all wear the same mood ring?" Lucien leaned over the table to take a close look. "Cool. Yeah, I still have Dad's. I stopped wearing it though because it always turned a strange red color. It was kind of creepy." He sat back in his chair. "What do you want with Dad's ring?"

Malachi and Stephen exchanged glances. Stephen was the first to speak. "When was the first time you saw it turn?"

"I don't know. About a year after dad died. Why?"

Malachi frowned. "You were only sixteen. That wasn't supposed to happen."

"What wasn't supposed to happen?" Lucien looked from Stephen to Malachi. "Somebody better start talking fast or I'm outta here."

Resting his elbows on the table, Stephen steepled his fingers. "Your father worked for an organization called The

Dream Keepers. We are all known as Dream Catchers. He was supposed to train you, but he was killed by a Dreamer before he had the chance. What you call a 'mood ring' is one of the ways we're alerted to their presence. Your ring should not have been active until your twenty-first birthday."

Lucien stared at the men with his mouth open. "I've heard Dad talk about this before. I thought he was losin' it. What are you guys into? What are you trying to get me into?"

Malachi sighed as he fingered his ring. "Sit back and relax, Lucien. You're about to take a trip to Wonderland."

Chapter 3

Monica walked into the game room, locked the door, and crossed the gleaming oak floor to the mantle. In sequence, her perfectly manicured fingers pressed the golden sleeping forms engraved in the frame of the mirror. She leaned into the bottom image and waited for the eye scan to finish its survey. The automated voice gave instructions to proceed with voice recognition.

"Dreamer, code 1967." The pool table in the middle of the room slid smoothly across the hardwood to reveal the stone staircase in the floor.

She descended the stairs, the rubber soles on her gym shoes muffling her steps.

The huge circular room was clear of any identifiable marks. The dismal gray stone walls held no decorations. One section of the wall was covered by twelve large computer screens. There were no clocks or windows. A dim bare bulb in the ceiling was the only source of light. A computer module and a rolling black leather chair were the only furniture.

Standing in front of the terminal, Monica tapped in the necessary codes. The room was further illuminated as The Legacy members came into view on the screens. All the women were stunning. Their tight flawless skin glowed with youth. They came in all shades and ethnicities. Thick shimmering hair in varying hues and lengths were their crowning glory. All of them could pass for women in their mid to late twenties. But most of them were only slightly younger than Monica. Two of them were barely older. Whether they met in person, or over the net they always used their Dreamer bodies. They all had served as Legacy members for years, an honor that was handed down from mother to daughter. Unless the member had no heiress, or her daughter proved to be unworthy. Then it was left up to the other Legacy members to vote on another candidate. "Good morning, ladies." Monica sat in the rolling black leather chair. "Everything has been set in motion. Somiar knows about Leila."

"Lider, does she know everything?" The Legacy member had a heavy Hispanic accent.

Monica addressed the member who had spoken. "Of course not. That would undermine everything we're trying to do. She knows just enough to get her on our side."

"Does she know about her father?" Another accented voice chimed in.

"No, I was able to come up with a cover story about him, but sooner or later, it's bound to come up again." Monica, realizing she was fidgeting, stopped drumming her fingers on the arm of the chair. "I'll start her training today. It will keep her occupied until we're ready for her to know the truth about him. She has already come in contact with someone close to the mark. I'll make sure she's where she needs to be, and when it's time, she will be ready to eliminate The Dream Catchers once and for all."

***

Somiar sat in the window seat of her old room and

watched as the gardeners pruned the rose bushes in the back yard. She used to love Atlanta in the spring time. Today, the sunny morning and the singing birds were like a slap in the face. How could the rest of the world go on, business as usual, when her world was falling apart?

She felt like an intruder in the room. The white silk curtains, the antique carousel horses, the ebony combs and brushes, every luxury a young girl could want belonged to the daughter of an heiress, not the freak she had become.

The knock on her door went unanswered. Somiar continued to stare out at the beautiful spring day, hoping whoever it was would go away. Her fingers curled tightly around the curtains, and her teeth clenched as the door opened. "I don't recall giving anyone permission to enter."

Somiar inhaled sharply when her mother entered the room. The upstairs housekeeper was usually the first face she saw in the morning.

Monica's black running suit and gym shoes gave her a younger look. Her gray hair was pulled back in a ponytail instead of her customary French twist. "Spoken like a true woman of power."

Hoping Monica would go away, Somiar turned her back and refused to speak. As far as she was concerned, Monica couldn't be trusted. Her sense of right and wrong was twisted at best.

"You can't ignore what you are, Somiar. It won't go away. Do you honestly think the Dream Catchers will let you be? They will find out who you are, and when they do, you'll wish you had never been born." Somiar tensed at the warmth of her mother's hand on her shoulder.

"I already wish I'd never been born." Somiar stood and turned, glaring at Monica. "How could you do this to me? How could you not tell me?" Somiar kept her grip on the fragile curtains, feeling the iron rod that kept them bolted in place give a little from the wall. "What kind of woman are you? I get here and learn I'm a freak of nature. You could have said something years ago. Am I supposed to thank you?"

Somiar didn't care if she hurt Monica's feelings. It was obvious to her that Monica never once considered the impact her lies might have had. Her nostrils flared. Everything she felt came out in a rush. "You're nothing but a liar and a killer, a freak in your own right."

Somiar's head jerked to the left. She tasted the blood in her mouth before it sank in that Monica had slapped her. Her hand flew to her face. She stumbled back from the fire in her mother's eyes. Who was the woman standing in front of her, hands clenched, the muscle in her jaw twitching?

"Put on some workout clothes and meet me downstairs in the gym in one hour. That's not a request." Monica stalked from the room and slammed the door.

Somiar hurried to her walk-in closet, eyes burning, cheek still stinging, and pulled out a sweat suit. She knew Monica would come back if she didn't comply. Monica had never raised a hand to her before and showed no remorse for having done so today. It was like looking into the eyes of a stranger. For the first time in her life, Monica actually scared her.

What happened to the carefree life she'd had yesterday? How had it all been destroyed in one night? Where'd my life go? I want it back.

As she descended the stairs and headed towards the gym she focused on breathing. Slow and deep, inhale and exhale.

She took a deep breath before turning the knob to the gym door with shaky hands she fought to steady. Monica stood on a mat in the middle of the massive, mirrored room in a different form-fitting black running suit, looking dazzling, and deadly. Somiar stood in the doorway unable to move.

"Come in and close the door." At Somiar's compliance, Monica continued. "If you're going to get Leila back, your training starts now. Come over here and hit me."

Somiar stared at her. "Are you crazy? I'm not going to hit you. You're sixty-five years old for heaven's sake. There's no way I'm going to hit an elderly lady."

"I've never been called elderly," Monica laughed. "Does this make you feel better?" The gray in her hair slowly faded replaced by blue-black, thick, silky strands, and grew out to a long braid down her back. The once mocha skin changed to the color of bronze. Gone were the lines at the corners of her eyes, the irises an eerie steel gray. Her body was toned and well-defined. She could easily pass for someone Somiar's age.

Somiar watched the transformation in fascinated horror. She couldn't tear her eyes from the creepy image in front of her. Her heart pounded and her stomach lurched. The urge to run from the room had to be fought down. Look at her. Don't turn away. This is what you are. "You're dreaming, aren't you?"

Monica touched a finger to her nose as if playing charades. "Dead on. I guess you were paying attention last night. Now hit me."

Wiping the sweat from her palms, Somiar took a step towards Monica and threw a halfhearted punch.

She cried out in pain when her arm was twisted, and she found herself flat on her back after Monica flipped her over her shoulder.

"You disappoint me, Somiar. Hit me. At least try this time."

She hunkered on all fours and jumped up, swinging at Monica with all her might. When she again landed on her back, she immediately got up, this time pissed off. She crouched and ran for Monica, planning to pull her legs out from under her.

When Monica spun around behind her and kicked her square in the butt, Somiar let out an indignant yelp.

"This isn't fair. You're dreaming." Somiar got back on all fours, breathing heavily.

Monica strode over to her and jerked her up by the collar. "You think you can do better dreaming?" Monica's voice was cold and angry. "Then sleep." Before Somiar could respond, Monica rammed a needle in her arm.

Somiar stared at her, eyes wide, and fell over before everything went black. When her eyes opened, she was again standing outside the gym. She shoved the door open, and found herself rooted to the spot. Monica was dragging her limp body across the shiny hardwood floor to a couch at the end of the room.

Trying not to let the sight faze her, Somiar strode to the center of the room, head held high. "Maybe now we can have a fair fight."

Monica turned and gave a slow smile closing the distance. "Then hit me."

Somiar thought back to her martial arts training. Monica had her taught by an expert since she was six. There were no belt colors, just levels. Somiar had always frustrated her teacher. He said she could be an expert if she just tried. But her heart wasn't in it. Now she was sorry. She got into fight position and took a swing at Monica.

Monica bent back slightly, easily avoiding the blow, and slapped her soundly across the face, drawing blood from her bottom lip. "Come on, Somiar, you're tough now, right? Both of us are dreaming, so stop fucking around and hit me." Monica ducked when Somiar swung at her again, then straightened and slapped her on the other cheek.

Blood spewed from Somiar's mouth, and she gagged at the metallic taste. She wiped her lips with the back of her hand and got back into fight position. Okay, Monica was serious, so she would be too.

Her effort was worthless. Every time Somiar swung, Monica ducked and slapped her, hard. The last time Monica hit her, Somiar sank to the ground, her left eye throbbing. "Stop it! I don't understand. Why can't I do this? This doesn't make sense." Somiar covered her stinging face with both palms and let her tears run over her fingers.

Monica gently moved Somiar's hands from her face. "Why doesn't it? Did you think that because you're dreaming you would gain some tactical skill you never possessed? Our world does have rules, Somiar. It also has its perks." She led Somiar over to the mirror covered wall.

Somiar gasped out loud at her puffy, bruised face. Her left

eye was blackened, and almost swollen shut. "Look at what you've done. I can't go out in public like this."

"You don't have to. Make it go away. Concentrate. What do you look like without the bruises?"

Somiar stared at her face, imagining the bruises fading away, and watched in amazement as they disappeared from her cheeks. The swelling around her eye shrank until it disappeared and the discoloration faded. "How did I do that?"

"You're a Dreamer. As long as you remember to heal certain injuries sustained during a dream state before you return to your body, they won't show when you're awake." Monica walked away from the mirror and sat in the center of the mat. "You can't change a deadly wound. If your dreamer body dies, so does your physical body."

"Can I look like anybody I want?" Somiar imagined several famous people in her mind and frowned when her appearance didn't change.

"No. Your Dreamer body has to be from your imagination." Monica tucked some loose tendrils back into her braid. "While we may come close to looking like someone, we can't pass as them. Some distinguishing feature would give us away. We also can't change gender."

"When do I get to meet The Legacy?" Somiar wanted to see what she was up against.

Monica rubbed the back of her neck, a habit Somiar learned long ago meant she was hiding something. "You don't. Nobody meets the Legacy except other members. I don't know who they are either. I always got my assignments through a heavily encrypted computer code. The code is indecipherable to anyone but a Dreamer." Monica jumped to her feet. "Enough of this. Break time is over. It's time I show you how to hit me."

***

Malachi and Stephen glanced up as Lucien entered the living room of his penthouse carrying a large wooden box. "My father left me this but I don't know what half of this stuff is. I guess you guys may be able to shed some light on them."

He flipped the lid, pulled out several items, and laid them on the white marble table. He pointed to the small, metal, star shaped pin. "Would one of you mind telling me what this is?"

Stephen picked it up and ran his finger over the crescent moon engraved in the top. "It's a dreamer pin. It renders a Dreamer unconscious, so they can't return to their physical bodies. It also has a tracking device, so we can find the sleeping body. We send those coordinates to the Keepers, and they use a different type of pin on the actual body causing them to rejoin. While the Dreamers are unconscious, we take them to a secure location." He carefully placed the pin back on the table. "The pins only work on Dreamers. If you stick a regular woman with this, you're either going to piss her off, or have her filing assault charges against you." He turned to Malachi and nudged him. "Isn't that right Malachi?"

"Screw you, Stephen. I only did that once." Malachi gave a hearty laugh at Lucien's astonished look. "Boy, was that woman mad at me. I had only been on the job for a few days and it was my first assignment. Young and way too eager to catch my first dreamer."

"You make it sound like it was no big deal. The woman thought you were trying to inject her with something."

Stephen collapsed against the cushions in a heap. His eyes watered.

Malachi thought Stephen was going to piss his pants from laughing so hard.

"Don't you remember, Mal? We had to erase her memory to keep her from going to the cops."

Lucien held up both hands. "Wait a minute. Erase her memory? And what do you mean if I stick someone? Are you expecting me to join this crazy group?" He shook his head. "Sorry guys, but this Catcher thing stopped with my dad. I just want a normal life, enjoying my inheritance."

"Unfortunately for you, being a Catcher isn't something you choose. You were born into it." Malachi chuckled at Lucien's horrified expression. He could relate to how Lucien was feeling right now. It was a lot to dump on someone all at once. "Believe me, I didn't like the news when I heard it either. As for erasing a memory, all it takes is a small dose of this." Malachi picked up what looked like an ink pen from the scattered items on the coffee table. "One injection and you can erase as much or as little of someone's memory as you want. Doesn't work on Dreamers or Catchers though."

Stephen leaned forward on the couch resting his arms on his knees. "There's still a mystery to solve here guys." He steered the conversation back to Lucien. "You said when you put your father's ring on for the first time, it glowed red. Did your ears ring?"

"What's that got to do with anything?" Lucien cocked his head to the side. "I kept having my hearing checked and the doctor said I was fine."

Malachi stood and paced the floor running a hand through

his hair. Something was going on. He was sure of it. It was one of the reasons he enjoyed being a Catcher. There was always some action or a puzzle to solve. The adrenaline rush he got from actually making a difference in a person's life was the best high there was. "It means you were in close proximity to a Dreamer." Malachi stopped and gave Lucien a sidelong glance. "I don't understand any of this. They never go after a Catcher if he's not a threat, but at that time, you weren't even a Catcher, so I don't get why your ring was active at such a young age. Most of us are trained by our fathers when we're teenagers but our rings don't activate until we're twenty-one." He stroked his hair stubbled chin. "And here's what really blows my mind. If they were close enough to activate the ring, they were close enough to kill you. Why didn't they? It couldn't have been you they were after."

"Wait a minute. You're trying to tell me that tinnitus and a glowing ring is an early warning system?" Lucien looked from one to the other.

Stephen poured himself a glass of water. "Not so early, I'm afraid. They have to be close enough to touch you before there's any warning. That's why they're so hard to catch." He took a sip from his glass and leaned against the bar. "You were marked to be taken out on your twenty-first birthday. You may not want a life as a Catcher, but it seems the Dreamers have made that decision for you. That's also why your training needs to start as quickly as possible. You're already behind, and they know who you are. We're taking you to the Dream Keepers today. They'll train you and assign your partner. They're also looking into possible reasons for you being able to activate your ring when you were so young."

Lucien almost knocked over the wooden box when he stood. "Taken out? Why would anyone want to kill me? What have I done?"

"That's what we're trying to find out." Stephen's voice remained calm. "Somebody wants you dead in the worst way, and we have no idea why. The Keepers had Malachi and I keep an eye on you. They were tipped off that you were in danger, but they don't know where the tip came from. As for the ring, it should have deactivated when your dad died. These rings only work on the fingers of Dream Catchers over the age of twenty-one. On anyone else's finger, they're just a useless piece of jewelry."

Chapter 4

Somiar sat at the dinner table pushing her food around her plate with a fork. Monica sat at the other end of the table, her food half finished. Apparently, the events of the last twenty-four hours hadn't affected her appetite. The silence in the room was unbearable. Somiar dropped her fork on her plate, the clatter breaking the silence. "Why do I have to be the one to save Leila?"

"Excuse me? Where did that come from?" Monica looked up from her dinner.

"It's a perfectly logical question. You're the one with the experience and training. Why do you need me to get Leila back?" Somiar narrowed her eyes. "I don't owe her anything. I didn't even know she existed until yesterday." How dare they put her into their fight? No explanations. Just, this is what you can do. Now go save your biological mother.

"She gave you life."

Monica's calm tone made Somiar want to scream. "I didn't ask to be here." Her voice shook with barely controlled rage. "And what kind of life did she really give me? From now on I'm doomed to be hunted for something I had no say over. Nobody asked me what I wanted. I didn't get a choice." She stood and leaned over the table. "Why should I risk my neck for her?"

Monica rounded the long dining room table and stood next to her. "You're the only one who can help her."

"Why?" The word came out like a hiss.

Monica offered her hand. "Come with me."

Somiar stared at Monica's hand like she'd never seen it before, refusing to take it. Holding her breath, and looking into Monica's eyes, she waited for some sign of emotion, any emotion from her. Her blood ran cold at her mother's blank expression. When Monica turned, leaving the dining room, Somiar silently exhaled and followed her up the stairs to the master bedroom.

There, Somiar realized Monica was a creature of habit. Like her study, Monica's bedroom hadn't changed either. The same four-poster bed stood in the same spot. The only difference was the comforter. Instead of the gold silk comforter that used to be there, a deep bronze one had taken its place. The vanity against the far wall was still there. She sat on the edge of the bed and remembered the times she would sneak into this room to imagine a mother who welcomed her. One that wanted her daughter to climb into bed with her has she read bedtime stories until she fell asleep.

Her memories were interrupted when Monica came to her and opened a black case containing a small platinum necklace with a ruby crescent moon pendant nestled on a bed of black silk. There was a black onyx star embedded in the middle of the ruby.

Monica lifted the necklace out of the case and hung it around Somiar's neck. "This belonged to your mother. She wanted me to give it to you. She said it would protect you from the Dream Catchers."

"It's beautiful. How will it protect me?" Somiar ran her finger over the onyx star in the middle of the pendant.

"According to Leila, as long as you wear it on your physical body, the Catchers won't be able to detect you. For some reason, it doesn't work on the rest of us. I tried it, and almost got caught for my trouble." Monica rubbed the back of her neck. "I don't know why it only works on you. Leila just made me promise you would have it if you ever had to face working for the Legacy."

Somiar's eyes met Monica's in the mirror. It was time she made herself clear. "I have no intention of working for the Legacy. After Leila is rescued, I'm done," she said with resolve.

Monica placed her hands on her shoulders. "You know you look just like her. I miss her so much." She turned from the mirror. "You need to stay here a little longer to complete your training."

It never ceased to amaze Somiar how Monica could change a subject so fast. Her words seemed rehearsed, like there were things she wasn't quite privy to. She knew more than she was letting on. Somiar was sure of it. "No," she said. Tomorrow I'm going home. I don't want to have to depend on being drugged to sleep. Tonight, I need you to teach me some natural sleep techniques and you have to teach me how to control where I go when I sleep. There's someone I need to see. I think he knows where Leila is." Somiar's palms sweat at the thought of seeing Malachi again.

Monica put her hands on her hips. "Are you sure you're ready for this?"

Somiar nodded. "Malachi Walker. He was there the night Leila was caught, and he knew I was a Dreamer." She fingered the necklace encircling her throat. "If this works, that won't be an issue tonight. I think he's the key to getting Leila back, or can at least point us in the right direction. I need to find him."

Monica went to stand at the head of the bed. "Come lie down." After Somiar got comfortable, Monica sat next to her. "Focus your mind on him. Since you don't know exactly where he is, you can't focus on a particular place or building, just him. You'll arrive at least in close proximity to where he is." A long pause. "Somiar, I feel it's my duty to give you the chance to bow out. At least for tonight. This is a dangerous game you're about to play." The gleam in Monica's eyes belied her words.

Somiar rubbed the fading bruise on her wrist. "You don't know the half of it."

***

Somiar opened her eyes in the bathroom stall of the Lunar Hotel lobby. Of all the places she could have ended up, next to a toilet wouldn't have been her first choice. She tried not to inhale too deeply before she opened the stall door and walked to the full-length mirror.

She inspected herself with a critical eye. The black knee-length backless dress showed off her curves to perfection. Her black spiked heels gave her long legs sexy definition, and made her ass look incredible. But the ruby crescent moon around her throat seemed out of place. Diamonds would add just the right touch. She smiled slowly as the platinum necklace faded, replaced by a three-tiered diamond choker. Her understated makeup and simple one carat diamond studs were just right. She ran her fingers through her brown shoulder-length curls and sauntered into the lobby.

She spotted Malachi coming off the elevator looking sexy as hell. His denim jeans accented his legs and butt. His black t-shirt stretched across his muscled chest and narrow waist. Her breath caught and her insides turned to liquid heat. She kept her stride steady and confident as she walked to the concierge desk so their paths would cross.

"Ms. Ayers?"

The deep baritone voice made Somiar's pulse race and her insides quiver. She let the sensuous feeling envelop her. "Mr. Walker. It's nice to see you again."

"Please, you can call me Malachi."

"I'll call you Malachi if you agree to call me Somiar." Somiar kept her face impassive as she watched Malachi take in her appearance. "Is something wrong? You're staring."

Malachi smiled. "I didn't mean to be rude. But you seem different from the last time we met."

"I was having an off night. I was on a date from hell, but everything's fine now." She gave a polite smile. She worked hard to keep her composure. The last thing she wanted was for him to think she was some half-wit fawning over him.

Malachi raised his brows. "Glad to hear it. Are you a guest here, or are you checking out?"

Somiar thought fast. "I'm having my condo renovated, so I thought I'd make arrangements to stay here while the work's being done." She handed the desk clerk her license and credit card, grateful to have something to do with her shaking hands.

"Well, it was nice to see you again. Please enjoy your stay." He gave a slight smile, and turned to walk away.

Somiar hid her disappointment at their encounter being so brief. Things weren't going as she planned. She was getting nowhere fast. She needed more time. "Listen, I'm meeting some friends for drinks later in the bar. Would you like to join me while I wait?"

"I'm flattered, but I already have plans for the night. Maybe some other time?" His gorgeous smile left her a little breathless.

She smiled back, hoping she wasn't showing too many teeth. "Sounds good. You can get my number from the concierge." Unable to think of a reason to hold him up, she turned to the front desk and made arrangements for a suite for two weeks.

She watched Malachi head out the door and pass by a stunningly beautiful woman. Somiar's eyes narrowed. The hairs stood on the back of her neck. Although the woman had changed her appearance, Somiar would recognize Monica anywhere. She had the stride of an alluring predator on the prowl. Her blue-black hair hung in loose spiral curls down her back with thin silver chains woven throughout. Her gray, tiger-like eyes held a mischievous gleam. The black silk halter top and tight silk pants made her body a moving work of art. The connection Somiar felt to her was almost palpable.

When Malachi passed Monica, Somiar could see the red glow from his ring. She opened her mouth to speak but stopped when Monica put a manicured finger to her red lips.

Her eyes widened when Monica pulled out a long dagger and threw it straight at her. The knife grazed her shoulder and embedded itself in the wall behind her. The stinging pain made Somiar cry out and instinctively grab her arm.

As Malachi raced to Somiar, Monica sprinted across the lobby and through the stairwell door.

Malachi checked Somiar's arm. "It's just a scratch. Stay here." Malachi ran after Monica.

Somiar yanked the knife from the wall, ran outside to the back of the building and willed herself back to her own body. When she opened her eyes, she turned her head to see Monica on the bed sleeping next to her. Somiar sat up and jumped off of the bed, not wanting to be near her.

Monica's sleeping expression gave Somiar a chill. Her lips were curved up in a slight smile, as if enjoying herself.

Somiar's hand went instinctively to her stinging arm, blood smearing her hand. Damn, I forgot to heal this. Somiar snatched the first aid kit from Monica's linen closet, then cleaned and bandaged her wound.

She was furious. If Monica was going to interfere, the least she could have done was let her know. What kind of person went around throwing daggers at people? Apparently, people she was now affiliated with. Somiar plopped down on Monica's chaise. The only thing she could do now was wait for Monica to wake up.

***

Malachi's feet pounded up the stairs as fast as he could move them. The Dreamer's heels clacked on the stairs above him and the steel door slammed shut on the next level. A few seconds later, he threw open the door and ran into the hallway.

Nothing. She was gone. The hallway was deserted. His heart pounded in his chest. He inhaled and exhaled slowly to control his breathing.

Somiar. The Dreamer attacked Somiar. He ran back down the stairs two at a time not wanting to wait on an elevator. She was nowhere to be seen. The concierge confirmed that Somiar had left the building.

Malachi ran his hand through his hair. "You, and I'm sure countless others, see a woman attacked in this building, and you let her walk out?"

"She didn't leave us much choice, sir. Security surrounded the building to protect you. We don't have the authority to hold her here."

"Did she leave her address or a home number?" Malachi concentrated on keeping his tone even. It was the man's first night on the job as a Watcher. Who knew he'd be confronted with Dreamers?

"Both, sir." He lowered his voice. "Should I alert The Keepers, sir?"

"Yes, and get Stephen Prescott on the phone and tell him to meet me in the penthouse ASAP." What the hell was going on? He rushed into his private elevator and pressed his thumb on the scanner. After his print was verified, the elevator jerked up towards the penthouse. As he came down from the adrenaline rush, he replayed the last few minutes in his head. His mind kept floating back to Somiar. Just the thought of her in that dress made him fantasize about what was underneath. The image of his hands ripping it from her body made his dick hard. Malachi rested his head on the cool metal of the elevator. Damn, where's your self-control?

So much for his relaxing night on the town. A new assignment had just fallen into his lap. He had to get Watchers assigned to Somiar and do a little damage control about tonight's incident. Then he needed to find out who had marked her, and why.

After entering his apartment, Malachi poured himself a drink. He was draining his glass when Stephen stormed in not letting Malachi get a word out.

"What's this I hear about a Dreamer being in the building? Who was the mark? What's going on?"

Malachi handed Stephen a glass of brandy and started to pace. "I don't know what the deal is. All I know is one minute I was talking to an...acquaintance and the next, a Dreamer was throwing a knife at her. We need to find out everything we can about Somiar Ayers. And we need to get Watchers to her address. Tomorrow, I'll pay her a visit and see if I can find out what's going on."

Stephen tapped the keys on Malachi's laptop, pulled up the hotel registry and printed out Somiar's information. "I'll talk to The Keepers tomorrow to see if they have anything on her."

"Stephen, the Dreamer was Rose."

"Black Rose?" At Malachi's nod Stephen let out a low whistle. "Oh man, I wonder who your girl pissed off. If Rose is after her, she may be as good as dead."

Chapter 5

When she noticed movement from Monica, Somiar sat up on the edge of the chaise. Before Monica could get a word out, Somiar started in on her. "You threw a knife at me."

"Yes, I know. I was there." Monica swung her long legs over the side of the bed and went to stand looming over Somiar. "And?"

Somiar recognized the attempt at intimidation. It was a tactic Monica had used on her before. But she was too pissed to fall for it. Rising to her feet, she stood toe to toe with Monica. "First of all," she held a hand up in front of Monica, "you need to back away."

Monica complied with a raised brow.

"It boggles my mind that you think this is okay. All I wanted to do was find him, maybe ask a couple of questions. I didn't expect to come out of it with a freaking knife wound."

"Stop whining." Monica leaned back against the footboard of the bed. "It's starting to irritate me. It got you what you needed. Now he has a reason to stick to you like glue. Just bat your eyelashes at him a few times, show a little leg, and he'll tell you anything you need to know."

Somiar went rigid. She couldn't believe what she was hearing. Her fists clenched so tightly, her nails bit into her palms.

"Gee, Monica, why don't I just screw his brains out? Maybe I'll get the information out of him a lot faster."

"If I didn't know you were being a smart-ass, I might think it was a good idea. Tomorrow you can go back to your condo, but two nights a week I expect to see you here. You can decide on whether you use your Dreamer body. Your training has to continue."

"Fine." Now that she had started this, she would see it through to the end. Her life was a mystery, and it was obvious Monica wasn't going to tell her all she needed to know. Leila was now her only hope.

Monica studied her, a smirk marring her beautiful features. "And don't get any ideas about Malachi, my love. This is not a game. If sex is on your mind, fine. But don't get attached. Remember, he will stop at nothing to see that you and our kind are eliminated. You may have to eliminate him first."

Somiar knew she didn't have it in her to "eliminate" anyone. But there was no way she was going to argue the point with Monica. In a few short hours, the woman had sent her on an unpleasant emotional rollercoaster. Instead, she changed the subject. "Don't you think you should have let me in on the plan? You could've gotten yourself captured or killed. And what was going on with that ring? How did he know you were a Dreamer?"

"If I had told you what I had planned, it wouldn't have been as convincing. You had to be caught off guard for the whole thing to appear real." Monica crossed the room and unpinned her hair. "You haven't learned to rein in your emotions yet. As for the ring, all the Dream Catchers have one. There's something about our Dreamer bodies that set those damn things off. Whenever we get too close to a Dream Catcher, those rings alert him to our presence."

"But I was dreaming too. Why didn't it glow when I was near him?"

Monica pointed to Somiar's necklace. "I guess it really works. Leila refused to tell me how. She just said it was imperative you had it for protection. Hopefully, she'll fill us in after you rescue her."

Somiar unclasped the necklace and studied it. It was beautiful, but she could find nothing special about it. "I told Malachi that I was having the condo renovated and I would be staying at the hotel for a couple of weeks. How long do we have before they revive Leila for interrogation?"

"I don't know. They may have already started. Leila's strong though. They'll never drag anything out of her. Problem is they aren't going to wait forever." Monica ran her brush through her hair, letting the thick silver strands fall to her shoulders. "But we have to act fast. If they don't get what they want, they'll kill her. We may not have much time."

Somiar absently ran her fingers over her bandaged arm. God, how could they be so cruel? They didn't sound any better than the Dreamers. "Malachi is probably going to have me checked out. Are you sure you can't be traced back to the Dreamers?"

"As far as the rest of the world is concerned, I'm just a woman with too much time and money on her hands. The only thing he'll find out about you is you're adopted. And don't worry about the condo. It won't be a problem for me to have someone on it whenever you need the work to start. Right now, we both need to get some rest. We're going to be busy until we get Leila back." Monica put her brush down and headed for her closet.

Somiar started for the bedroom door.

"Somiar?" Monica's voice stopped her and she turned. "Don't go back out tonight."

Refusing to respond to her mother's request, Somiar clamped her lips together and left the room, slamming the door behind her.

***

Somiar pulled several items from her closet and hung them in wardrobe boxes marked for the hotel. After filling her suitcase with lingerie, she went back into her living room and surveyed her surroundings. Absolutely no color. Everything in the condo was beige, white, or taupe. Nothing was out of place and everything was spotless. It was downright depressing. When did I become such a tight ass?

She walked out onto her balcony overlooking Piedmont Park and watched the joggers and children at play. With her hands braced on the stone rail, she closed her eyes and enjoyed the gentle spring breeze caressing her face carrying the scent of lilacs to her nose. The park was beautiful this time of year. The grass lush and green, magnolia and dogwood trees in full bloom. After her morning jog, she usually took a walk in the Botanical Gardens next to the park.

Her mind drifted back to a simpler time, only days ago. A time when she was ignorant of how she touched the lives of other people while she slept. Ignorant of the fact that the blood of assassins ran through her veins. Ignorance is bliss. Somiar had never believed that, until now.

The whine of an engine forced her out of her moment of

serenity. She glanced down to see several workmen climbing out of a large van, canvas covers and boxes in tow. Somiar left her balcony and opened her door for the bustling crew.

When Malachi stepped over the threshold behind the workmen and grabbed her hand, she inhaled sharply. "We need to talk. Where's the bedroom?"

"What are you doing here?" Somiar snatched her hand away from him, hoping he wouldn't notice her sweaty palms. "Are you some kind of stalker? Leave or I'm calling the cops."

Malachi scowled. "I'm wondering why you haven't already. Someone threw a knife at you last night and you don't seem at all concerned."

Somiar's mouth went dry. Damn Monica and her bright ideas. She was hoping she wouldn't have to deal with him until she moved into the hotel. When several of the workers shot nervous glances their way, she lowered her voice. "How do you know I didn't call the police?"

"Because none came to the hotel after you disappeared." Malachi glanced around the room at the workmen. "Now do you want to tell me what's going on right here, or in private?"

She motioned to one of the workmen. "Go ahead and start covering the furniture, I'll be with you in a moment." Somiar turned to Malachi. "Follow me." He knew she wouldn't talk to him in front of the work crew and it pissed her off. Too many people were calling the shots in this cat and mouse game, and not one time had she gotten to play the cat.

Straining to calm her raw nerves and slow her heartbeat, she closed her bedroom door. *Good Lord, the things I could do to this man in this room.* Forcing her mind back to the business at hand, she gave him what she hoped was an unwelcoming glare. "What are you doing here?"

"Why haven't you called the police?"

She played with the handle of her hair brush and narrowed her eyes. "I asked you first."

Malachi sat on the edge of the chaise in the corner of the room. He appeared uncomfortable on the low seat with his knees bent at a sharp angle. His tall, muscled body practically dwarfed the small couch. "Listen, I know who attacked you last night, or rather, what attacked you. What I don't know, is why. Until we find out who's behind this, I'm putting you under my protection."

Now that didn't sound unpleasant at all. As a matter-of-fact, being under anything of his sounded pretty damned good. Somiar struggled to keep her voice harsh. "You're not putting me under anything." She stood abruptly, the brush falling to the table. "What's all this we stuff anyway, and what do you mean you know *what* attacked me? I don't know you from Adam, and you don't know me." She stopped in front of him, hands on her hips. "How dare you come barging into my home, questioning me? You run a hotel, not my life." Her glance settled on the bulging muscles in his chest. Realizing she was way too close to him, she took a step back. "Are you crazy or something?" Somiar hoped the anger in her voice covered her hurt feelings. She didn't like being referred to as a what.

Malachi rubbed his chin. "How did you know I ran the hotel?

Somiar rolled her eyes, "Who doesn't? It's the most exclusive hotel in the city and your name and picture has been plastered all over the travel section of the paper."

"Why didn't you call the police?" Malachi's voice remained calm.

"Why didn't you?" At his blank stare, Somiar hid the smile of triumph that tugged at the corners of her lips. No way would she play her hand first until she was sure she would come out the winner. "I don't owe you any explanations. None of this is any of your business. Just stay out of it." Somiar closed her eyes and pinched the bridge of her nose. "Please leave."

Malachi stared at her. "What are you hiding? Who are you trying to protect?" His voice was almost a whisper.

"This conversation is over." Somiar opened the bedroom door and waited for Malachi to leave, her emotions at war. She wanted him to stay, but needed him to go. If only they'd met under different circumstances, maybe things could have been different.

Malachi stood and loomed over her. She could feel the heat from his body. The spicy scent of his cologne made her want to bury her nose in his chest. "Look, whoever did this is trying to kill you. Those people aren't hired to scare or intimidate. Their only function is to kill. They're vicious, evil predators who know nothing but death and destruction."

Somiar felt the heat on her face. He talked about her people like they were scum. Not all Dreamers were killers. They couldn't be. She'd never killed anyone, and didn't plan to. Still, she was what he hated, what he thought of as vile and vicious. The reality that they were destined to be enemies weighed heavily on her. Somiar turned her back to him, and stalked to her front door, the curious gaze of the workmen following her progress. The sound of Malachi's footsteps wasn't far behind.

Taking care to keep his voice down, Malachi put his hand on her shoulder. "You're in danger, dammit! Don't you value your own life?"

"Why do you even care? Get out." Somiar kept her face composed, and opened the door.

Malachi walked out the door and turned. "Whoever you're protecting, they're not worth it."

Somiar slammed the door in his face. Leaning against the door, she closed her eyes and concentrated on her breathing.

"Ma'am? Would you like us to start packing up?"

Taking a deep breath, she turned to the contractor. "Of course. Let's start with the kitchen."

***

Monica took her place in the center of the room, smiling proudly at the faces of The Legacy surrounding her on the monitors. "Good afternoon, ladies. I have some good and bad news." Her discovery was still fresh in her mind as she greeted the women. "First, the good news. I have confirmed the necklace works. The Dream Catcher could not detect Somiar." Monica ran her hands over the arm of the chair, her smile fading. "However, we have a problem I didn't expect." She dug her fingers into the fabric. "I couldn't sense her either. I only recognized her because she hadn't changed her appearance."

"The necklace blocks Catchers, and Dreamers?" The Italian member, Iris, seemed stunned.

"Unfortunately, it does." Monica bit her lip, "but Somiar

could still sense me. She knew who I was when I walked in the door."

The Russian member, Rain, spoke up next. "Have you discovered why it works on just Somiar?"

Monica swiveled her chair in Rain's direction. "No, but Leila does, and we have our suspicions, but she will have to confirm. We need to get her back."

"She will never go along with our plan. She will not sacrifice her child." Violet's heavy Austrian accent cut in.

Monica bit her lip. "No, she won't, but we don't need her. If our suspicions are correct, all we need is Somiar. Leila betrayed us long ago. Once we confirm how the necklace works, she will be eliminated."

"And how is the young Dreamer's training coming along, Lider?" Dahlia's lilting Indian accent chimed in.

Monica kept her voice steady. "She's learning fast. Her physical endurance is unmatchable. Her biggest obstacle is her emotions. She hasn't learned to reign them in yet, but I'm making progress. I'll make a true Dreamer of her yet. She's discovering that her emotions will bring her nothing but trouble. She will learn to fake it, as I have." Monica lifted her chin. "As we all have."

"What about Lucien?" Dahlia asked.

Rage bubbled inside her and the pulse in her temples throbbed. Monica leaned forward in her chair. "The little bastard got away." Her hands gripped the armrests. "But the Catchers can't hide him forever. Sooner or later, he has to face the real world." Monica abruptly cut the connection to the rest of The Legacy.

Closing her eyes, she concentrated on breathing and slow-ing her pulse. Lucien was a big thorn in her side. There was no telling what he was capable of. His existence could mean the end of the Legacy. She would eliminate him if it was the last thing she ever did, and Somiar was the key. Monica didn't know how much longer she could hide her real agenda from the Legacy. Her perfect control over her emotions was slipping. It was time for her to retire. Being a Dreamer didn't mean she would never age. Nor did it mean she'd never get sick. The chemotherapy and radiation didn't work. She was going to die, and she needed a successor. It was time for Somiar to take her place as Lider Somini, The Dream Leader.

Chapter 6

Somiar followed the bellman through the door of her hotel suite and surveyed her surroundings. The plush chocolate-colored sofa scattered with colorful throw pillows, beckoned her. All she wanted to do was sink into its softness, and drift into a dreamless sleep.

Her lips twisted at the thought of a dreamless sleep. Her dreams now defined her, made her unique. With sleep would always come the reminder of what she was. One night of fantasies that belonged to just her and touched the lives of no one would be a blessing. A blessing most people took for granted.

After tipping the bellman, she pulled off her shoes and let her feet sink into the thick beige carpet before moving to the large picture window. The Atlanta skyline against a twilight backdrop would have been breathtaking, had her mood not been so somber. Tonight, it mocked her. Now, she saw it through the jaded eyes of a Dreamer and wondered if she would ever see anything as beautiful again. The ugliness of what her life could become, what she was expected to become, took the beauty out of life.

A haunting sense of loneliness filled her as she tried to figure out where she would go from here. How many Dreamers were out there? How many didn't know who or what they were? She resolved to fix one thing at a time. She closed her eyes and rested her fingers on the cool window. First Leila, then answers.

The ringing phone interrupted her thoughts. She picked up the receiver and lounged on the couch, settling into the cushions. "Hello?"

"Somiar, I trust you're finding your accommodations acceptable?"

Malachi's voice was deeper than Somiar remembered and her stomach fluttered at the sexy rumble. Hearing her name come from his lips made her clench her knees together.

She inhaled, taking care to remove the receiver from her lips, so he would not hear her unsteady breathing. "Malachi. I won't ask how you knew I was here. What can I do for you?"

"I need to see you. I have some information you need. There are things going on you know nothing about, things you may not even believe." Somiar did a mental victory dance. Monica's ploy worked like a charm.

"Anything you need to tell me, you can say now." She kept her voice even and casual. If he suspected she wanted to see him just as badly, it would make him suspicious. And that could spell disaster.

"Not over the phone. I need to see you privately. Either you can come to my suite or I can come to yours."

Somiar bit her lip. The thought of being alone with him made her heart skip a beat. "I'm afraid neither of those choices are acceptable. I was planning on going to the Roman Room for dinner in a few minutes; you can meet me there. And Malachi, this had better be good. I don't like wasting my time."

She hung up the phone and went into the bathroom to

check her makeup and hair. Her tangerine silk dress exposed one shoulder. Thank God Monica had taught her to always look her best even if she were just making a trip to the grocery store.

When her thoughts drifted to Monica, Somiar felt a stabbing sense of loss. They had never been close, but there had always been a degree of respect for each other. That was in the past. Somiar had lost all respect for her. She'd been lied to for twenty-five years, then treated as if it were no big deal when the truth came out.

But she felt a sense of duty to a race of people she knew very little about, and she didn't know why. Perhaps it was a sense of self-preservation. They were her people and Monica was right about one thing. She couldn't hide from what she was.

She gave herself a mental shake, then grabbed her purse and headed to the dining room.

Somiar stood framed in the open smoked glass door of the dining room trying to remember the story she had rehearsed on the elevator. The columned room was brightly lit with several crystal chandeliers. Subdued murmurs from patrons engaged in conversation and the tinkling of silverware and crystal glasses made the room almost merry. Silver silk material draped from the walls and ceiling, accented with colorful bouquets on pedestals softened the square shape of the room.

Malachi was easy to spot. Although he was at a private table in the back corner of the room flanked by massive columns, her gaze automatically went to his as soon as she walked in. She instantly knew where he was. She could almost feel him. The thought unnerved her. What was it about this man that made her temperature rise while she simultaneously broke out in a cold sweat every time she saw him?

Monica's words came back to her. If sex is on your mind then fine, but don't get attached.

She lightly ran her tongue over her lips. Oh, the possibilities.

Squaring her shoulders, Somiar headed toward him with confident steps across the gleaming marble floor. Confidence she didn't feel.

***

Malachi watched Somiar cross the room. There was something almost feline about her, something primitive and dangerous. And sexy as hell. His gaze traveled from her long legs to where her nipples strained against the sheer material of her dress and his mouth actually watered. The diamond pins scattered throughout her hair enhanced her regal beauty. He stood when she approached the table and held her chair.

With a challenge in her eyes she sat and crossed her legs. "Good evening, Malachi. Where's the fire?"

Malachi took his seat and tried to ignore the sense of déjà vu. The nagging sensation that he had seen her somewhere before still irked him. He motioned to the waitress. "Ms. Ayers and I will need a little more privacy. I'll let you know when we're ready to order."

The waitress gave a small nod. "Yes sir." She stood back and pulled the braided cord behind Somiar releasing the tied back silver curtains.

Malachi pretended not to notice Somiar's stiffening posture. "Have you given anymore thought to what I said?"

"About you protecting me?" Somiar took a sip from her water glass and shook her head. "No. It's creepy. Why should I trust you anyway? I barely know you." There was a tremor to her voice. What the hell was she so nervous about?

He pulled a photograph out of his jacket pocket and placed it on the table, never taking his eyes from her.

"What's that?" She lowered her eyes to the photograph.

Malachi slid the picture across the table. "Do you recognize this woman?" He watched her closely and saw a glimpse of surprise in her eyes before they went blank again. She was hiding something, and he was determined to find out what it was.

This was the part of the job he usually hated most. Telling people he had to protect, what they were in for. He had a feeling that he would regret it when the time came for her memory to be erased.

***

Somiar couldn't hide her surprise as she gazed at Monica's picture. What was Malachi doing with it? How could Monica be so careless? There she was, plain as day in a restaurant. Somiar didn't recognize the man Monica was with or the background. Of course, Monica had changed her appearance. She looked the same as the night she threw the knife at her.

When she glanced at Malachi and saw the interest in his face, she knew she had given herself away. Monica stressed at every training session how important it was to control her emotions. One slip could mean her life. Somiar silently vowed to do better. "How could I forget her? She threw a knife at me." The disdain in her voice was not an act.

Malachi gave an impatient sigh. "Okay, Somiar. What's going on, and I want the truth."

"You first. Who is she and why are you carrying her picture around? You seem to have more explaining to do than I." Somiar hoped she sounded convincing.

Malachi sat back and studied her for several seconds. Somiar refused to turn away. No way was she going to let him think he had the upper hand unless she wanted it that way.

He leaned forward and gave Somiar a stare so intense, a chill ran down her spine and goose bumps rose on her arms. She fought the urge to rub them as he started his tale. "The woman in that picture is known as Black Rose. She's part of a group of specially trained assassins hired by the ridiculously wealthy, and they're excellent at their jobs. They're almost the perfect weapon. They kill and leave no evidence behind. If this woman came after you, then you've been marked."

"I don't understand. What does this have to do with you? If these people are as good and dangerous as you say they are, how can you help me?"

"I'm a Dream Catcher. I work for a group called The Dream Keepers. It's my job to make sure these people are caught and kept from doing harm. These are not ordinary people. They kill while they're asleep." Malachi talked slowly, like a man talking to a child.

Somiar tried to act as if she didn't know what he was talking about. "What do you mean they kill while they're asleep? Are you trying to tell me that there are a bunch of killer sleepwalkers on the loose?"

Malachi gave and exasperated sigh. "They're called Dreamers and no, that's not what I'm saying. Have you ever heard of out-of-body experiences?"

Somiar nodded. "Of course."

"That's how they operate. While asleep, they are able to leave their physical bodies and interact with people who are awake. Unfortunately, they can also change their appearance, so they're almost impossible to identify."

"Yeah...right." She stood on shaky legs. It wasn't his story that unnerved her. It was him. Something in her craved to be near him. Made her want to tear his clothes off and taste every part of him. She decided to use her raw emotions to her advantage. "I think I'll have dinner in my room. Call me when you have a meeting with Santa Clause, or the Easter Bunny. It was not so nice seeing you again, Malachi."

Malachi also stood and grabbed her wrist. The glimmer in his eyes was almost desperate. "Just hear me out, please. Your life depends on it. If you don't let me help you, you're a dead woman."

Her skin tingled at his touch. His words made her heart thump in her chest, but she was not afraid. An almost uncontrollable urge to pull him close and kiss him senseless came over her. His voice was a natural aphrodisiac. Forcing her pulsing body to heel, she tried to summon what she hoped was fear in her eyes. "That sounds like a threat. If you don't take your hands off me right now, I swear I'll scream the place down." Somiar let her voice rise slightly, wanting him to take her threat seriously.

Malachi released her and held his hand up. "I'm no threat to you. Just listen to what I have to say. After all, a woman," he picked up the picture, "this woman, did try to kill you. I know it sounds unbelievable, but I can help."

Somiar backed against the curtain, letting her gaze dart around the enclosed space as if looking for an escape.

"Please, Somiar."

His plea made her tremble. What would her name sound like, rolling off his tongue while she had him under her?

Shoving the thought aside, she hesitantly returned to the chair and secretly applauded herself for such a good performance. She also felt a little guilty for being so manipulative. "Okay, I'm listening."

"I've been working for the Keepers for years. I know how Dreamers operate and I've saved several lives since. My job is not to take your life, but to save it." He ran a hand through his hair and gave an exasperated sigh. "Think about it, Somiar. I know when you checked in and what room you're in. If I'd wanted you dead, you wouldn't be here right now. Assassins aren't interested in cat and mouse games. They cut right to the chase. You get marked, you're dead. That's where I come in."

Somiar fidgeted. She didn't expect to be intimidated. If she didn't know better, she'd be petrified. "So, you're going to kill her before she kills me, is that it?"

He steepled his fingers. "That depends on her. I won't kill her unless it's necessary. If possible, I'll just put her out of commission. If I can catch her alive, I will."

Somiar saw her chance to gain some ground on Leila's location. "Where do you keep the Dreamers once you catch them? I mean, can't they just dream their way out?"

He sat back in his chair. "We keep them in an induced coma using special equipment, until we're ready to talk to them. It keeps them from dreaming. As a matter of fact, they are aware of nothing."

He sounded proud of himself. She clenched her hands together in her lap and tried to keep the hostility out of her voice. "How many have you caught?"

Malachi rested his chin in his hand. "Why do I get the feeling you're trying to avoid telling me what's going on with you? I've told you what you need to know and now it's your turn."

Somiar moistened her lips and recited the cover story she and Monica had concocted. "I was adopted when I was a baby. My adoptive mother is an extremely wealthy woman and I stand to gain everything when she passes away. Unfortunately, money brings all kinds of scum out of the woodwork." She let her gaze wander to her lap, unable to meet his eyes while telling a bald-faced lie. "My life was good, until I started getting threatening calls. I don't know who this man was, but he started making crazy demands. He insists that we be married and I would find out who he was only when I agreed and not before."

After taking a sip from her glass, she inhaled deeply and plunged back into her story. "I thought it was a joke. I didn't take it seriously until I was faced with someone throwing a knife at me. I think she," Somiar said tapping the picture with her nail, "was sent as a warning."

She watched a myriad of expressions cross Malachi's face ranging from surprise to disbelief.

"You have to believe me. I know this sounds ridiculous, but he actually hired someone to kill me!" Somiar forced desperation into her voice.

"So that's why you didn't call the police." Malachi returned the picture to his jacket pocket. "Somiar, you have to let me protect you. I know how to handle people like this. I've dealt with them before." His voice lowered. "They won't stop until you're dead or give in to their employer, and trust me, if he can afford to hire a Dreamer, you're dealing with a man with a lot of power."

The sincerity in his voice made Somiar sorry she had to deceive him this way. She wanted to come clean.

"The Dreamers are vermin," he said. "If I could, I would destroy them all."

Somiar cursed herself. No coming clean or letting her guard down. No more would she let her emotions control her. "I would be grateful for your help." But inside she seethed. He saw her as nothing more than something filthy to scrape off his shoe after he squashed her. Monica was right. The Dream Catchers were definitely her enemies.

Chapter 7

Somiar followed Malachi into the elevator. Her brows drew together when she saw there were only three buttons that read Lobby, PH27, and PH 28. The two penthouses in the hotel. "Wait." She reached out to hold the door open. "I'm on the wrong elevator."

Malachi brushed her hand away and, when the doors closed, pressed his thumb on the scanner. "No, you're not. My partner keeps twenty-seven for when he's in town and you're staying with me in twenty-eight." He ignored her indignant gasp. "I can't protect you if I can't see you."

"I'm not staying with you." Somiar ignored the tingling between her legs. He suddenly felt too close. She leaned back against the wall, and took care not to let her fingers curl in a death grip around the chrome handrails. Her heart wouldn't stop its irregular beat. How was she supposed to think straight with him around?

"For heaven's sake, Somiar, I have an extra bedroom. You can stay there. I'll have housekeeping bring your things up." She didn't like his mocking tone. It made her feel like a prude.

Somiar stepped forward, hands on her hips. "Oh no you don't, buster. If you think I'll have tongues wagging about being your next conquest, you've got another thing coming."

"I have no intention of making you a conquest, or anything else, except a client." He folded his arms across his chest and pinned her with his gaze.

Somiar didn't know whether to be disappointed or insulted. "It still doesn't seem right. I'm not staying with you." She tried to keep her nerves out of her voice.

"Newsflash, it's the twenty-first century. No one cares who's staying in a hotel room with whom. It's not like we're celebrities." His lips twitched, trying to stop a smile. "And I certainly didn't have you pegged as the type who cared what other people thought."

"If you're such a great judge of character then maybe you should have figured out that I don't like being told what to do."

Malachi's grin widened. "I knew that, but you're awfully cute when you're annoyed."

She felt the warmth on her cheeks and tried to stop the involuntary smile. Malachi could be charming when he wasn't putting Dreamers down. She didn't want to like him, but couldn't help it. "Fine, I'll stay." She turned toward the elevator door, keeping her back to him. Every nerve in her body was aware of him. What was she going to do? Having him this close all the time wasn't part of her plans.

The elevator doors opened to short hallway with large oak double doors at the end. Malachi pressed his thumb on the scanner embedded into the wall on the left of the doors, then inserted a black card into the lock. When the door opened, he moved aside to let Somiar enter first.

She stepped over the threshold and surveyed the penthouse. Everything was black leather and stainless steel. "You don't have very many visitors here, do you?"

He frowned. "Why do you say that?" He walked past her and kicked off his shoes.

"There's nothing warm and inviting about this room. Nothing on the walls. You don't even have a plant." She re-surveyed the room, trying to find something, anything that gave some clue to who he was, what made him tick. She hoped he wasn't as cold as the room.

He shrugged his shoulders, "I don't want anything around that needs to be taken care of."

It didn't sound like his remark was directed towards her, but it made her wonder. She crossed her arms. "Then why am I here?"

Malachi turned away from her. "Because it's necessary. Follow me. I'll show you to the guest room."

"But you said you've handled people in my situation before. If that's the case, surely I can't be the first client you've had here." Somiar trailed behind him, a little annoyed. It always riled her to have to talk to someone's back.

"Well, you are." Malachi opened the double doors to the guest bedroom.

When he came to a sudden stop, she almost ran into him. She followed his line of sight to the king-sized bed but found nothing that should hold his attention. "Is something wrong?" She circled around him and tossed her purse on the bed.

He dragged his gaze from the bed to her face. "Excuse me, you were saying?"

Somiar gave him a sideways glance. What the hell was wrong with him? "I want to know why I'm here."

He took a deep breath. "The Dreamer that came after you

is very important to the Catchers. We've been after her for a long time. I thought you'd be safer here."

She worked hard to keep her expression neutral and prayed not to give herself away. "Why is she so important? What makes her so different from other Dreamers you've encountered?"

"That's not your concern." His tone left no room for argument and Somiar seethed. He sounded too much like Monica.

Somiar walked slowly toward him, eyes narrowed. "What's going on, Malachi? And I don't want to hear that you don't need to know bullshit."

He turned to the door. "I'll have your things here in a few minutes."

She stepped in front him and put her hand on his chest. "What's going on?" Her breath caught at the shock in his eyes.

***

Malachi sucked in a deep breath when Somiar put her hand on his chest to stop him. Everything went hazy. When his vision cleared, the scenery in the room had changed. There was a picture of two little boys and a girl on the vanity. A blue glass vase filled with white lilies stood on the bedside table. His attention wandered back to the bed. He saw the same picture he had seen when he first opened the door. There they were, lying together naked, bodies sweating and entangled. The feel and scent of her sweat slicked skin made his muscles tense. What the hell was going on?

In the blink of an eye the room flashed back to normal. Malachi backed away from Somiar and gently moved her hand from his chest. "Later. We'll talk later." He was taken aback at the loathing in Somiar's eyes before she slammed the door in his face. She seemed to have a bad habit of doing that.

Walking to the front room proved to be difficult. His dick stood at full attention. What was it about this woman that always gave him a hard on? Sure, she was beautiful, but so were a thousand other women in Atlanta. His mind struggled to make sense of the scenes playing around in his head. She'd felt so real. For those brief seconds, he could hear, feel, smell and taste her.

Man, I need to get laid. It had only been a few weeks. What the hell was happening? He was fantasizing like a teenager about a woman he knew nothing about. This shit just didn't happen to him, there were too many women willing to share his bed.

He'd never led anyone on. It was no secret that he planned to stay single for the rest of his life. That was something he always made clear. Unfortunately, most women seemed to think that was some kind of challenge. He didn't know why they insisted on trying to be the one to change his mind and shackle him to them for life. The minute a woman got too clingy, he cut her loose. There was no room in his life for deep relationships, especially in his line of work.

He poured himself a drink and called housekeeping to have Somiar's belongings transferred. Something told him he'd better watch his step with this one.

***

Somiar stepped out of the shower and ran a towel vigorously over her body. How dare Malachi dismiss her like that? She went into her room and jerked a black tank top over her head and pulled on her black silk boxer shorts. Sitting at the vanity table, she roughly ran a brush through her thick brown hair and secured it with a clip.

She was sick of the bullshit. Why were people treating her as if she was on a need to know only status when it came to her life? She paced the floor, too wired to sleep. Her mind raced, and she tried to turn it off but her angry thoughts would not be quieted.

She had to get out of this confined space. She opened the door and crossed the living room floor to the kitchen. Her lips split into a smile when she peered into the refrigerator. Well at least he keeps his fridge stocked. After pulling out a beer, Somiar popped the top and settled down on a bar stool at the kitchen island. Tipping the bottle to her lips, she willed her mind to slow down, concentrating only on the ice-cold brew sliding down her throat.

Unfortunately, her thoughts continued to get in the way. There were too many things that didn't add up. Monica knew what she was but didn't tell her. Why would she do that? Something about the story didn't ring true. Was Leila really after a Dream Catcher at the club that night? And was it a co-incidence that Somiar and Monica was there at the same time? Somiar took another sip from her bottle. Something wasn't right.

"Now there's something I don't see every day."

Somiar choked on her beer at the unexpected deep voice. Launching into a coughing fit, she grabbed a napkin and held it to her lips until the coughing stopped. Then she pressed a hand to her chest and took several deep breaths, trying to stop her heart from pounding. "Dammit, why did you do that? I hate it when people sneak up on me."

"I didn't sneak up on you, I walked in here the same way I always do. Excuse me for not stomping around my own home." Malachi nodded at her beer. "Mind if I join you?"

Somiar shrugged. "Your kitchen, your beer." She couldn't help but notice the muscles bulging under his t-shirt and her pussy jumped. Crossing her legs at the ankles and clenching her thighs she hoped her discomfort didn't show. Sure, he was hot, but damn, it wasn't like she didn't see bodies like his every day. Atlanta was full of sexy, dark chocolate men. Although they were tempting, this was the first time she wanted to throw one on the table and fuck his brains out.

She watched his lips as they touched the tip of the beer bottle, wondering what those lips could do to her.

Malachi rested his elbows on the table, and slowly peeled the label off his beer. "You can tell me to mind my own business if you want, but I have to ask. Do you always wear men's underwear?"

Somiar grinned. "No. I just think they're comfortable to lounge around in." She eyed his jeans and t-shirt. "Don't you ever sleep?"

It was his turn to smile. "Sure, I do. I guess it's just a little hard for me to sleep knowing someone else is here."

Somiar absently ran her finger over her bottle watching the condensation drip onto the stainless steel counter top. "I guess it could be unsettling if you're used to being alone." When he didn't respond, she glanced up to see him gazing at her absent caress of the wet glass. She lifted her beer and drained the bottle, ignoring his heated stare. "You know, now would be a good time for that talk you promised me." Somiar hoped the change of subject would quiet the lust threatening to boil over in her. "What's so special about the woman in the photograph?"

Malachi took another drink of his beer and took a deep breath. "I suppose you have a right to know." He moved to the refrigerator pulling out two more beers. After popping the tops and handing one to Somiar, he returned to his seat at the island. "The woman after you is the deadliest Dreamer the Catchers have ever come in contact with. She's killed several Catchers, including a friend of mine. We've been after her for years."

Somiar wasn't sure she wanted to hear the details of Monica's dirty work, but couldn't stop herself from asking questions. She had to know. "I thought you said all the Dreamers were good at their jobs. Why is she so much deadlier?"

"Because she's never missed. The night she came after you, she didn't want you dead. She couldn't have. You were an easy target." He sighed heavily and massaged the muscles at the nape of his neck. "Apparently, her employer hasn't given the order to kill you yet. We've never been able to keep any of her marks alive. That's why I want you here."

Somiar cleared her throat and stared down at her hands, now clasped in her lap. "She killed a friend of yours? How did you know it was her? I thought you said Dreamers changed their appearance." Monica didn't do it. Somiar kept repeating the phrase in her head. It had to be someone else. Please, God, let it have been someone else.

Malachi stood, almost knocking over his stool, and stared out his balcony window. "She's gotten so confident, she started leaving calling cards. There's always a black rose found on or near the body. She wants us to know it was her." The frustration and anger in his voice made Somiar wince. "It's like she's laughing, daring us to catch her."

Black roses. Her mind drifted back to the strange flower arrangement in Monica's study. A large arrangement of black roses with one white rose in the center. Her heart plummeted. She leaned over, taking deep breaths, fighting the bile that threatened to rise up and spill from her lips. Pull it together, Somiar, just pull it together. "Do you know who hired her to kill your friend?" She couldn't keep her voice from shaking.

Malachi didn't seem to notice. The moonlight highlighted his clenched jaw, the muscle slightly twitching. "I have no idea. He was about to retire, so he was no threat to the Dreamers. They didn't have to kill him."

Her breath caught. No wonder he hated Dreamers.

He sounded as if he were no longer with her. He was reliving the past. "One morning he was found in a grave yard, a dagger in his chest and his tongue cut out. The Catchers have kept an eye on his son since then. He has no one else." He leaned against the wall and gazed at Somiar through hooded lids. "If anything happened to Lucien, I'd never forgive myself."

Somiar let the tears escape from her eyes. How could Monica do this? How could she so savagely murder someone? This was no ordinary hit. It sounded personal. Somiar felt his pain in her heart. At that moment she knew she could never live the life of a Dreamer. As a matter of fact, she could see herself fighting against them.

She went to him and rested her cheek and palms on his chest, closing her eyes. "What was he doing in the graveyard? Does anyone know why he was there?"

Malachi's body tensed at her touch. Wanting to ease his pain, she ran her hands over his arms and back, trying to loosen him up.

She felt so guilty about Monica being the cause of so much anguish.

Malachi's voice shook. "We can only assume he was visiting his wife. He was found on top of her grave. I'd never met Leila, but I was told he loved her with all his heart."

Somiar stepped away from Malachi. "What did you say?"

"What's wrong? You look like you've seen a ghost." Malachi's brows drew together, his confusion plain.

Dreamers can only have one child, and they are always girls. Somiar replayed Monica's words. It had to be a different Leila. "Was Leila Lucien's natural mother?"

Malachi's smile was uncertain. "That's a strange question. Why do you ask?"

The question barely registered in Somiar's brain. "Huh? Oh... just wondering. I guess when you're adopted, questions like that seem natural." She held her breath, waiting for his answer.

Malachi arched a brow. "If you say so. As far as I know, Leila was Lucien's natural mother. I never asked. By the time I met Richard, Lucien's father, Lucien was fourteen."

Somiar silently exhaled. If Leila was Lucien's mother, there was no way she could be hers. As unlikely as it seemed, he was talking about a different person. Or someone was lying. "How did she die?"

"In an explosion at their house. Gas leak. Luckily, Lucien and Richard weren't home. Lucien was just a couple of months old at the time." Malachi went back to the kitchen and threw the empty beer bottles in the trash.

He turned back to Somiar. "You must be exhausted. Go ahead and get some sleep. Tomorrow we'll visit my partner and figure out where to go from here."

She saw the pain in his eyes. Her questions stirred up bad memories for him, and she wanted to make them go away. Maybe, in the comfort of his arms, she could forget her own fate. At least, for a little while. So what if it only lasted one night? One night was more than she could have hoped for a few hours ago. Closing the gap between them, she placed a gentle palm on his cheek. "I'm not tired."

She stood on her toes and placed a soft kiss on his chin, the stubble from his beard lightly pricking her lips. When he didn't move, she gazed up into his eyes, the pain replaced by surprise.

Coming off her toes, she removed her hand and lowed her gaze to the floor. "I shouldn't have done that. I'm sorry."

He put his fingers to her chin and lifted her face to his. The desire in his eyes unmistakable. "Are you really? I'm not."

Somiar put her hand to his chest and felt his heart pounding. "No," she breathed. "I'm not sorry."

He softly put his lips to hers, and ran his hand down her back. Slowly, his tongue traced her lips. Barely touching her mouth with his, he inhaled deeply. His full lips covered hers, his arms wrapped around her waist pressing their bodies together.

She tried to savor the anticipation of what was to come but her body's desperate need for him wouldn't be ignored. She deepened the kiss, sliding her tongue into his mouth, tasting the beer on him. His muscular arms engulfed her and made her feel safe and secure.

When he slid his thigh between her legs, she trembled. She tore her lips from his and rested her forehead against his chest, breathing heavily and trying to get a hold of herself.

Malachi was still as a statue. He kept his arms around her, sensing she needed the support. His masculine scent was intoxicating. It reminded her of the first night she met him. All that was missing was the sweat. The thought of his sweaty naked body made her press herself more firmly against his thigh. Her need for him continued to grow. She surrendered and stopped trying to contain it.

Bringing her lips back to his, she pulled his t-shirt out of his jeans and jerked it over his head. The sight of his perfectly cut chest and arms made her immediately wet. She entwined her arms around his neck and lifted her legs, wrapping them around his waist.

Sliding his hands under her ass to hold her up, he took her to his bedroom, kicking the door shut.

Somiar slid to her feet and pulled the clip from of her hair tossing it aside, not caring where it landed. When her hands went to the clasp on his jeans, his hand covered hers. She looked up, hoping the desire in his eyes hadn't faded.

The heat in his gaze was intense. "I can't make you any promises."

Somiar withdrew her hand from his grip and lifted her tank over her head. "I'm not asking for any."

Malachi pulled her back to him and crushed her lips under his. He yanked her silk boxers down below her hips and let them drop to the floor.

"Does this mean I can pick up where I left off?" A slight smile teased her lips at the sight of the huge bulge in his jeans.

"By all means." His voice was deep and sexy.

The familiar spasm between her legs made her hasten her movements. Her fingers worked on the button at his waist while she ran her tongue in small circles around his nipples. His hardened nipples and the salty taste of his skin against her tongue made her long to taste the rest of him. But she wanted to let him take the lead.

He ran his hands through her hair and gently urged her head back as he kissed her lips fiercely. She moaned against his mouth, her body tingling, wanting to feel his hands everywhere at once.

Malachi turned her around and held her back against him, his hard dick pressed against the top of her ass. His soft kisses on her neck made her want to melt where she stood. One hand traveled over her breasts teasing her swollen nipples one at a time making them tingle. The other slid down her stomach and between her legs. Somiar lifted her leg and rested her foot on the side rail of his bed to allow him better access. Her breath caught and her body quivered as he slid his fingers in and out of her wet pussy then circled her clit.

Her sensitive fingers teased his lips. He captured each one in his mouth, teasing them with his tongue. Somiar's eyelids lowered to slits.

As Malachi plunged his fingers deeper inside her, she let out a moan and felt herself going over the edge. Not willing to come without him, she pulled his fingers away from her and turned back to face him. She put his fingers in her mouth and tasted herself on them.

Her hand wrapped around his rock-hard dick and stroked him with long, smooth strokes. She threw her head back and stared into his eyes. "I want you. Now." The fire in his eyes consumed her. He laid her on the bed and positioned himself over her.

"Now, Malachi." She didn't care if she sounded demanding. Her body wanted him, and she wouldn't deny herself tonight. Nothing else mattered.

He plunged into her without gentleness. Closing her eyes, she let waves of pure pleasure wash over her. She didn't need love and tenderness right now. She wanted her primal lust satisfied. As her heart pounded, she could hear her blood rushing in her ears. She wrapped her legs tightly around his waist and tightened her muscles around him pulling him deeper inside her. Her fingers stroked his hair as she pulled his head down until their lips met, tongues sliding together. Her hands glided down his sweat slicked back. This was the smell she missed.

His moans and growls sounded far away to her. He put his arms under her back and hauled himself to his knees, bringing her with him, her legs still around his waist. She threw her head back, turned on even more from the sweat dripping from his face down her chest.

Now that she was in control of the pace, she planted her feet on the mattress and moved faster, slamming herself against him, until she could feel her stomach flutter. Her pussy contracted uncontrollably around Malachi's dick and Somiar knew there was no stopping her climax no matter how hard she tried. "Malachi. Come with me. I can't hold it anymore."

Malachi wrapped his arms tight around her waist and thrust himself into her as far as he could go. He held her in place, a long growl escaping from his throat as he exhaled. His body shook, muscles taught, their bodies locked together.

Somiar felt the liquid warmth seep into her body. Her muscles slowly relaxed. She nuzzled her face in Malachi's neck, waiting for her breathing to return to normal.

Malachi pulled the top sheets back, then laid Somiar on the bed. "We're going to freeze when we cool off." He pulled the sheet up to cover them both and stretched out beside her.

Somiar turned over and sighed in contentment when he spooned her body. She liked the way he felt up against her.

He kissed the back of her neck. "Any regrets?"

Somiar barely heard him. "None." For the first time in a long while, she drifted off into a dreamless sleep.

Chapter 8

Malachi woke in an empty bed and sat up in confusion. He ran a hand over his eyes, thinking back to the night before. How long had he been alone? Glancing at the bathroom door, he listened carefully for running water. The realization that Somiar wasn't in the room disappointed him. Waking up next to her would have been a pleasant way to start the morning.

Throwing his muscular legs over the side of the bed, he stood and stretched, fighting the urge to find Somiar and bring her back to his bed. Instead, he strode into the bathroom and turned on the shower.

Standing under the hot water, he wondered how she would act this morning. Hopefully, she hadn't left his room regretting their night together. He'd spent too many 'morning afters' with guilt ridden lovers. Then there were the 'I wonder if I slept with him too soon' women. Maybe he shouldn't have let things go as far as they had. He certainly didn't want things to be awkward between the two of them. Their situation was precarious enough.

After putting on a pair of jeans and a black tee shirt, he opened his bedroom door expecting the worst, but hoping for the best.

He heard Somiar before he saw her. Her back to him, she poured a cup of coffee, ear buds in, singing, "If I Were a Boy."

And she was singing it badly. The song was barely recognizable. She definitely was no Beyonce.

Trying not to startle her, he cleared his throat with a loud, "ahem." His attempt failed miserably. He watched her wiggle her ass, her white flared mini skirt swishing while she sang. His lips twitched in amusement until he could no longer contain the laughter bubbling from his lips. Struggling to control himself, he leaned on the breakfast bar, settled his chin in his hand and kept his eyes fixed on her gyrating butt.

When she finally turned, she gasped and jumped back, dropping her coffee cup. "Why do you keep doing that!"

Malachi straightened, still laughing. "I tried to let you know I was here." Realizing she couldn't hear a word he said, he walked around the counter and tugged the earphones from her ears his fingers brushing her face. "Maybe you shouldn't wear these while you're here. I have the annoying habit of sneaking up on you even when I don't mean to." His gaze roamed from her eyes, filled with longing, to her slightly parted lips.

"Where's your broom?" She backed away and laid her iPhone on the counter.

"In the closet behind you." He decided to let her avoidance pass without comment. There was no point in pursuing the matter. Obviously, last night had bothered her. It would be best to let her handle it in her own way. Of course, if she wanted a repeat performance, he wasn't going to turn her down.

He opened the refrigerator and pulled out bacon, eggs and cheese. "I thought I'd whip up an omelet. Would you like one?"

Somiar wrinkled her nose. "No. I hate eggs. I think they're an ingredient, not a main dish." She dumped fragments of the broken cup in the trash and filled another cup with coffee. Settling on a bar stool, she stared at him over the rim of her cup before setting it on the counter. "Listen, about last night."

Malachi continued beating eggs in a metal bowl with a wire whisk. Uh-oh. They were about to have 'the talk.' "What about it?"

"I don't want you to get the wrong idea." Lowering her eyes and fiddling with the handle of her cup, she nervously continued. "My life is really complicated right now and there's no room for a relationship."

The silence that followed was deafening. He let the whisk drop into the bowl. "Relationship? I don't recall any conversation about a relationship. I told you last night I wasn't making any promises." He turned to the stove, placing a pan on the burner, hoping the regret wasn't apparent in his voice. His own life held no room for a relationship either, but still, her rejection was a blow to his pride. He wasn't used to being on this end of the talk.

"Good. I thought you should know." She sounded relieved.

After he poured the eggs in the frying pan, he leaned in close to her. It was time to turn the conversation around. "Last night was good. We didn't do anything wrong, we needed each other." He ran his knuckles softly down her cheek, then a finger across her lower lip. "And now that we know where we stand, why don't we simply let this be what it is."

"What is it?" Her voice, almost a whisper.

"Two people, making the most of a bad situation."

She ran her tongue over her lips, grazing his finger, her gaze never leaving his. She closed the distance between them and brushed his lips with hers. Pulling away she gave him a small, slow smile. "You're going to burn your eggs."

"Damn." He yanked the pan of the stove, and fumbled around trying to save his breakfast. "I just want to make one thing clear. I didn't bring you here with the intention of sleeping with you." Placing his plate on the counter, he sat, straddling a bar chair. "I've never slept with a client before."

She smiled. "That's good. I've never slept with an employee."

Sitting across from her, he was again struck by the eerie feeling they'd met before. He studied her face, trying to force the memory to the surface.

She kept trying to look everywhere but at him; above his head, off to the side of him, she was even fidgeting in her seat.

"Do I have something hanging out of my nose?"

The question caught him totally off guard. His brows rose. "Excuse me?"

"You're staring. Do I have something hanging out of my nose? If I do, just say so. Sitting there staring at me is kind of creepy."

"I keep having this strange sense of déjà vu around you. I've seen you somewhere before, and not just in passing."

"We've never met before I ran into you at the restaurant." Throwing a coy smile his way, she ran a finger over his hand. "I would have remembered."

What the hell was going on with her? It seemed she was

trying a little too hard to convince him. He withdrew his hand from the table, and frowned. "What are you hiding?"

"I have nothing to hide. Why are you so paranoid?"

Was she actually getting defensive? Tapping his fingers on the table, Malachi gazed at her face. Either she really believed what she said, or she was a damned good liar. Loud rap music blared from his cell phone, interrupting his thoughts. After glancing at his phone, he slid his thumb across the screen. "Talk to me, Stephen." He went into the bedroom without a backward glance at Somiar and closed the door.

"Hey, Mal. On my way to see Lucien. I want to make sure he's not driving the Keepers crazy."

Something in Stephen's voice raised a red flag. "That's not what you called to tell me." Malachi sat down. Whatever it was, it had to be big. Stephen wasn't the type to stall unless he had to be the bearer of bad news.

"I got the information you wanted on Somiar Ayers." The long pause that followed made Malachi uneasy. He'd known Stephen long enough to know there was something he didn't want to tell him.

"Well," Malachi said with an impatient sigh, "are you going to tell me what's up, or do I have to beg?"

"I tracked the sources and checked her background, and for the most part, she's pretty clean."

"Good deal. I've got her staying here with me." Malachi waited for the lecture he was sure he had coming. Stephen had been a Catcher much longer than Malachi, and it pissed him off that he was sometimes treated like the rookie he no longer was.

"Is that really necessary, Mal?" Irritation sharpened Stephen's voice. "What do you know about the girl?"

"I know she's being hunted by the most dangerous Dreamer we've ever encountered. And you know as well as I that she wouldn't be safe anywhere else. No Dreamer can get in this place." Malachi didn't like his decision being challenged. Not under these circumstances. He wanted this particular Dreamer caught more than any other.

Stephen's voice rose a fraction. "I think you rely too much on the catcher stones, Mal. They'll keep that weirdo out of your place, but are you going to keep the Ayers chick there forever?"

Malachi rose from the bed and paced the room as Stephen's words sank in. How could one woman make him loose focus? If he were honest with himself, he couldn't blame everything on Somiar. His need for revenge ran deep. The monster clawing after her owed him a life. Richard had been more than a friend to him. He had been like a father.

Lost in thought, Malachi had almost forgotten Stephen's last statement. "Just tell me what you learned, okay?"

"Not much. She was adopted and her mother is a very wealthy woman. Owns several resorts here in the States and a couple in the Caribbean. They all cater to the obscenely rich. Somiar has a master's in business and is being groomed to take over." Again, Stephen paused.

"Okay, I sense a 'but' coming on." Malachi held his breath waiting for the other shoe to drop.

"Listen man, this could be nothing, but I had to bring it up. I think you should ask Somiar about her name. Find out who named her."

Malachi frowned. "Come again? Why would I need to know about her name?"

"Because Somiar, is the Catalan word for dream."

Chapter 9

Somiar sat at the kitchen island letting her mind wander back to the previous night. It wasn't like her to sleep with a man so fast. She was no virgin, but neither was she loose. There was something about Malachi that drew her to him. It wasn't only his face and body, though both were outstanding. She felt connected to him. One thought of him and her whole body screamed for her to take him and leave all her inhibitions behind. It was as if her body recognized him.

But why was he so sure they had met before? The first time she had laid eyes on him was at the hotel club, and even then, she had changed her appearance.

Her cell phone buzzed, interrupting her wandering thoughts. When she saw Monica's likeness on the screen she sighed, in no mood for an inquisition this morning.

"Hello, Monica. This is not a good time." Somiar couldn't keep the impatience from her voice. After all this was over, she would put as much distance as possible between herself and Monica. She had been saving money since she was a teenager and had quite a tidy sum in the bank. Of course, she wouldn't be able to live as extravagantly without Monica's backing, but she didn't care. Monica's money seemed dirty to her now. She didn't want to know how much blood paid for her to live as carefree as she did.

Monica didn't seem to notice Somiar's abruptness. Either she didn't notice or she didn't care. "What the hell happened to you last night? You were supposed to get here and put in some training time. You could have dreamed your way here."

Somiar glanced anxiously at Malachi's closed door and stepped onto the balcony, keeping an eye out for him and lowering her voice. "Listen, I can't go popping in and out of here. Sooner or later, he'd get suspicious and I'd get caught."

There was silence on the other end of the line. For a moment she thought the call had dropped. "Monica? Are you still there?"

"Yes, I'm here." Monica sounded irritated as well. "Fine, your training will resume once you get Leila. Just remember what you've learned and for heaven's sake, don't go anywhere without the necklace."

"Fine." Somiar went back into the penthouse and put her phone in her purse just as Malachi re-entered the room.

"Who were you talking to?"

"My mother. I didn't tell her what was going on and I want to keep it that way. I don't want her to worry about me." Somiar studied Malachi's face. She didn't like the way he was looking at her. Was that suspicion in his eyes? What had she done now? "Is something wrong?"

Malachi sat on the couch and leaned back. "That depends on you." He steepled his fingers. "I never asked; how did you get such an unusual name?"

Somiar furrowed her brow and licked her lips, still unsure of what she had done. "My name? My mother gave it to me." She smiled at the thought. "My little dream. That's what she used to call me." It was the only time Monica had ever used a term of endearment for her. Now she had to wonder if there was something else behind the nickname.

"Did you know that your name is the Catalan word for dream?"

"Of course. The language of love. My mother loved Catalonia. She raved about it so much that I vacationed there for a summer. I wanted to see what all the fuss was about." Her mind drifted. She'd had the time of her life during that trip. It was also the summer she had lost her virginity. "Why the sudden interest in my name?"

"I find it a strange coincidence that you're being hunted by a Dreamer," he said in a deceptively calm voice, "and you bear that name. I also can't figure out why a man you claim to know nothing about wants you so badly." He stood and crossed the room stopping inches from her. "Of course, you're desirable," he brushed his fingers lightly up and down her arm. "But not many men would stoop to murder or hiring a Dreamer just to claim a wife."

Somiar slapped his hand away. "If you're trying to make me feel like a cheap slab of meat, you're succeeding."

"It can't be your money." He kept on as if she hadn't spoken.

Had it not been for the glint in his eyes and his slight frown, she would have thought he hadn't heard her.

"Anyone who can afford to hire this particular Dreamer has to be wealthy already." He raised his hand and lifted Somiar's chin, forcing her to meet his gaze. "What is it that he really wants from you?"

"Why don't you ask him when you catch him?" His lips were too close to hers. Just a little more and the tingling craving of her own lips would be satisfied. How the hell did he do that? He could have her running cold then hot in the space of a few seconds. Trying to clear her head, she backed away from him until her legs came in contact with the coffee table.

Malachi dropped his hand. "As you wish. My partner will be meeting us later on today. Right now, he has business to attend to."

Fighting the urge to satisfy her craving, Somiar went back to the kitchen and started clearing the dishes, aware that Malachi's gaze never left her. The deafening silence was grating her nerves. "What do you say we get out of here today? I'm starting to go a little stir crazy." She lifted her gaze to his. "Maybe we could go for a walk. How about the Botanical Gardens?"

"I don't see the harm. Just stay close."

Staying close to him didn't sound unpleasant, and the thought of getting out, lifted her spirit. She had spent only one night with him, but the walls were closing in on her. She wasn't used to always having someone around. And someone as sexy as this man? Too much of a distraction. She needed some wide-open space, some distance. It would be lovely if they could have a fling with no strings attached, but she had an agenda, and so did he. It all came down to who got what they wanted first. "No problem. Maybe we can go to Screen on the Green tonight at Piedmont Park. I don't know what's playing, but it could be fun." Her enthusiasm died at the disapproving glimmer in his eyes.

"My partner is coming to see us tonight, remember?" He grimaced. "Somiar, your life is in danger. If we can save you, we might have a chance of catching the most sought-after Dreamer in history."

Great. He wanted Monica and she wanted Leila. Everybody wanted someone. But no one wanted her. If only he knew. She was the key to what he wanted most. Revenge. Though her heart ached for him, she would not be a means to an end. She would be the only one to walk away from this with what she wanted. Wouldn't she?

Chapter 10

Somiar tilted her head back and welcomed the fresh floral scent surrounding her. Pulling the pins from her hair, she closed her eyes and let the scented air lift it from her shoulders. The Botanical Gardens had always been her favorite place, and spring was the perfect time to visit. Bright colorful flowers against multicolored foliage. A little piece of Eden in the center of the city.

"Beautiful." The word was a whisper carried on the wind.

She opened her eyes to meet Malachi's gaze. Nothing in his face suggested he had spoken. "Did you say something?"

"No, nothing." He suddenly became very interested in a group of lilies on the side of the path.

"Come on. Let's look around." Somiar strode over to him and put her arm through his. "You'll love the canopy walk. It's almost like walking through the treetops. And I've spent a lot of time in the Japanese garden. The serenity has always given me a sense of peace."

Malachi glanced her way. There was a hint of sadness to him. "Serenity and peace. That means a lot to you, doesn't it?"

She stopped to inspect a deep red, trailing plant. "It's important at times. But how interesting would a lifetime of serenity and peace really be?" She let the crimson blooms and green leaves wind between her fingers. "I don't think the human brain could handle it. We tend to need a little drama, a little adventure to make our lives worth living. You ever read Jack and the Bean Stalk?"

Malachi paused next to her. "Can't say that I have, but I know the story." His eyes sparkled with amusement.

"A full-sized man in a land of giants. Have you noticed that all fairy-tales are filled with danger and conflict?" She strolled past him, the spring air parting the split in her sundress giving him a good view of her thigh. "I loved fairy tales when I was a child. The princess in distress, the handsome prince, the evil villain."

Malachi laughed, then widened his stride to catch up to her, capturing her in his embrace. Her enthusiasm was apparently contagious. "The handsome prince and the beautiful princess always win, but I don't think they were in 'Jack and the Beanstalk."

It felt so good to be in his arms. Somiar rested her cheek against his chest wishing this feeling, this moment in time could last. She leaned back to see his face and smiled. "Hmm. If I had written it, they would have been."

Hand in hand, they explored the rose garden. Monica's garden would have put this one to shame. The scent from the huge, beautiful blooms had greeted her every morning from her open bedroom window and lulled her to sleep at night. A sense of sadness and loss overcame her when she came to the pink tea roses. They were always her favorite, and her childhood home was full of them. She used to love to visit that part of the garden in her free time. Surrounded by pink roses and her favorite book. She leaned over a perfect pink bloom and inhaled deeply, letting the scent take her back.

Malachi came up behind her and put his arms around her waist. "Where are you, Somiar?" She barely heard him. His body warmed her back. Though she could hear the smile in his voice, his breath on her ear made her close her eyes in anticipation of what could come later. Pulling away wasn't an option. It felt so right, so natural. This was the way things were supposed to be. She wanted to let herself believe in the beautiful lie of the moment. But the truth would not be denied. He could never be hers, and she could never be his.

"I never thought I'd be the star in my own personal horror movie." She didn't mean for the words to slip out. This time was supposed to be relaxing. A way to help her unwind. It was her reason for picking this place. She withdrew from his embrace. This was no fairy tale. This was her life. And it wasn't fair. So many lives would be affected by the decisions she made. Hers, Malachi's, Leila's, and Monica's.

He stepped in front of her and placed his warm hands on her shoulders. "I won't let anything happen to you. She's not going to get away with this, and neither is the person responsible for hiring her. Trust me." The determination and concern in his eyes made her heart melt. She brushed a soft kiss across his lips.

As soon as she did, one name came to mind. Judas. It was she who couldn't be trusted. She was the liar, the manipulator, the fake. She was going to betray him. There was no other way. One long survey of his eyes told her all she needed to know. He would do whatever it took to protect her.

"No." Backing away from him, she shook her head. "You're putting your life on the line and I won't let you." She sprinted past him down the path, her sandals clacking against the concrete. Knowing she couldn't outrun him, she slowed her pace and turned. Apparently, he knew she couldn't get away from him either. He had not moved. He just stood there staring at her as if stunned.

The distance between them gave her a moment of clarity. Choose. Her mother or him. If she chose her mother, he would go back to his life hunting Dreamers, including her. And he would hate her.

Choose him and she would have to come clean. After taking her down, and what was left of her family, he would go back to his life, hunting Dreamers, minus her. And he would hate her. What choice did she really have? She had to protect her family.

She took a step toward him when a hand clamped around her mouth, jerking her head back, and her feet left the ground. Despite landing hard in the foliage on one shoulder, Somiar kicked her assailant back into the trees and crouched on all fours.

"Idiot! Where did you think you were going? Time is running out. Leila is as good as dead." Monica's voice came from the underbrush. She tossed a heavy piece of parchment at her, then ran through the thick trees, Malachi in pursuit.

Somiar sat up and drew a deep breath. Fingers shaking, she opened the paper. *This is your last warning.*

Chapter 11

Malachi slammed his fist on the counter top. "Dammit, Somiar. This guy's for real." He picked up the note and rammed it at her. "Does this look like a joke to you?"

Somiar rested her head in her hands. Her mild headache had become an intense throb. "No, it doesn't." It didn't seem like a joke at all. Monica was serious. She still had no clue about Leila's location. Leila is as good as dead. What was that supposed to mean? "What do you want me to do? I don't know how she knew I was going to be there."

"Your phone." Malachi held his hand out. "Give me your phone."

"What? Why?" She pulled out her phone and handed it to him.

"Most cell phones have a tracking device installed. Especially the expensive ones." He took her phone and pulled it apart. "If this Dreamer is as good as I think she is, all she has to do is hack into your phone records, get your info, and she can track you anywhere." He went into the kitchen with her phone and threw it in the trash compactor.

"Hey! Are you fucking crazy?" Somiar ran in the kitchen and glared at him. "Do you have any idea what that was worth?"

"Didn't you hear a word I said?" Malachi practically yelled

at her. "From now on, no more little field trips. I can't believe I let you talk me into this one."

She stood and glared at him, hands on her hips. "Why do you insist on blaming me for everything?" She advanced on him, until they were toe to toe. "Some crazy man is stalking me. My fault. My mother gave me a weird name. Again, my fault. That lunatic snatches me today." Somiar slapped her palm to her temple, widened her eyes and spoke in a goofy valley girl accent. "Oh my God, what was I thinking? That's my fault too."

"I'm not kidding." The vein in his temple pulsated so hard, Somiar thought he would have a stroke.

"What do you want me to do? I have no control over what's going on here." *You're such a liar.* Afraid her guilt would show in her eyes, she turned away from him and forced the thought from her mind. It wasn't like she got to pick her mother, or the woman who adopted her. She never asked for any of it. Rage bubbled to the surface. Malachi was the only one she could take her anger out on. "I'm sick of all this shit. My choices were taken from me, and I'll be damned if I'll let you or anyone else make me feel like any of this is my fault." Whirling back toward him, she jabbed her finger at his chest, and ranted on. "I refuse to be the helpless victim here. Let's do what we have to do to get what we want and be done with it."

"And what do you want?" The words were soft and gentle. The anger in his eyes had turned to curiosity. "Tell me what you want. When this is over, what will you leave with?" He tilted his head to the side, his lips so close to hers, she could feel his words on them. "You said people aren't content with peace and tranquility, so what will you take with you?"

The loud music from Malachi's phone saved her from having to answer. Malachi drew back and slid a finger over the face of the phone. "Talk to me Stephen." After listening for a few seconds, he pulled the phone from his ear. "Somiar, Stephen's here and needs to talk to me privately. I'm just going to go down to his apartment for a moment. Could you excuse me for a while?"

"Whatever." She knew her attempt at sounding casual failed miserably. "I'm tired anyway. I'll nap for a bit." Somiar went to her room and shut the door. She'd recognized Stephen's ring tone from earlier. If she was going to spy on Malachi, now was as good a time as any. She pulled open her middle drawer and reached under her clothes, fingers closing around the long velvet case. When she secured the clasp, the necklace lay cold against her skin. Although nearly weightless, it felt like an anvil around her neck, a painful reminder that she was about to commit the ultimate betrayal.

Lying down on the soft bed, she forced herself to relax and controlled her breathing the way Monica had taught her. Inhale. Toes, calves, knees, and thighs relaxed. Exhale. Abdomen, fingers, and palms relaxed. Inhale. Chest, neck, and head relaxed. Exhale. Mind clear. Her thoughts focused on Malachi as her eyes fluttered closed. Her body became a weightless mass.

She opened her eyes when her feet touched a hard surface, a soft breeze caressing her face. The balcony she found herself on was identical to Malachi's only this one had plants of all colors and sizes on it. A small, white, wrought iron café table and matching chairs stood in one corner. The deep voices coming from the other side of the sliding glass doors barely reached her ears. Taking a step closer, she bit her lip to keep from crying out at the small shock that stung her fingers when they came in contact with the door. Strange. Static was something she didn't expect her Dreamer body to experience. Besides, the balcony was concrete. Pushing the sensation from her thoughts, she pressed her body against the door, and listened through the glass and heavy cream-colored drapes.

"Man, you're not going to believe this one. You remember the Dreamer who was after Lucien? She wants to speak to you, and The Keepers are interested in finding out why." Somiar couldn't place the male voice. She guessed it had to be Stephen's.

"Well, that's new." The acid in Malachi's voice was hard to miss. "Listen man, can't you go? I don't want to leave Somiar upstairs by herself."

"No can do. She says she'll only talk to you. It's a long shot, but maybe we can find out who marked Lucien." Stephen's voice was slightly familiar. Where had she heard it before? "I'll stay with the girl. Just watch your back. You never know what a Dreamer's going to pull."

"Will do. Got to go let Somiar know what's going on first. I'll brief you on the meeting when I get back."

When Somiar heard the front door open she closed her eyes and returned to her body. She rose from the bed and started at the knock on the door. "Just a minute." With nervous fingers she reached behind her neck and fumbled with the clasp on her necklace then tucked it back in its hiding place and opened the door.

Malachi was standing near the front door, keys in hand.

"Listen. I have to make a run. This is my partner, Stephen Prescott. He's going to stay with you while I'm gone."

Somiar glanced at the handsome older man. He appeared to be in his mid to late thirties, despite the smattering of gray hair at his temples. It only added to his good looks. He was slightly shorted than Malachi, but equally muscular. Good grief. Were all the catchers built like well- trained athletes?

"Nice to meet you ma'am." When Somiar limply shook his hand, he smiled. "Don't worry. I'm harmless."

"I'm not." Never one to immediately trust a stranger, Somiar wasn't sure she liked him yet. She ignored Stephen's quirked brow and condescending smile and turned to Malachi. "Where are you going?"

"I have some business to attend to. I shouldn't be gone longer than a couple of hours." He took her chin in his fingers and gently tilted her head up, so she would have to look at him. "You'll be safe with him. I promise to hurry, okay?"

At her mumbled acceptance, he stepped over the threshold. She watched him until the door closed, blocking him from view. The emptiness inside her at his departure caught her off guard. This had to be over soon. If not, she was sure she would lose her head.

Chapter 12

"What's she like?" Malachi strode with Luke down the empty hall of The Keepers Center. He never liked being in this place. Although he wasn't claustrophobic, knowing they were seven stories underground made him feel closed in. The fluorescent lights shining on the white walls and floor made every tunnel seem identical. A person could get lost in these halls if he didn't know where he was going.

Luke was head of the Atlanta-based Dream Keepers Council. His thin, tight dreads were always braided together into one single braid that hung to the center of his back. His neatly trimmed mustache and beard showed just a hint of gray. "She's not much different from any other Dreamer I've interrogated. But I never expected her to go asking for you. Any idea what that's about?"

"None." Malachi stopped at the white doors to Luke's office. "Ready?"

"I'm as curious as you are. Let's get this show on the road." Luke opened the door and let Malachi walk through first, then leaned against the closed door.

Malachi took in the gleaming black hair above the blue suede back of the chair. Leather restraints encircled slim wrists. Manicured hands rested on the arms of the chair. He came to rest on Luke's desk, one leg dangling just above the floor. Her smooth complexion reminded him of melted caramel, her full lips stretched into a grimace. But it was her eyes that captivated him. Light brown and piercing, her lashes thick and black as coal. And he had seen her somewhere before.

Hers was not the face from the night club. As he thought, she had changed her appearance that night.

"Malachi?" Her husky voice was also different. "I didn't think they would send you."

"You have exactly ten minutes, Dreamer." Malachi folded his arms in front of him. "What do you want?"

She licked her lips and took a deep breath. "I believe you knew my husband and son."

"Just like a Dreamer." He narrowed his eyes and rested his hands on the sides of the desk. "Liars. The bunch of you. We already know you can only spit out your own kind. You can't even bear sons." He started for the door. "I'm not in the mood for your games." Malachi motioned for Luke to step aside. He had no intention of leaving, but she didn't have to know that.

Luke stepped forward. "Time to go back on ice, cupcake. No sweet dreams for you."

"My name is Leila; my husband's name was Richard. Our son is Lucien." The desperation in her voice stopped Malachi in his tracks.

It couldn't be. Gooseflesh rose on his arms. He stepped back around to the front of the chair and studied her face, recognition washing over him like a bucket of cold water. His brain couldn't make sense of what he saw. What the hell? His mind knew one thing, but his eyes were telling him something totally different. Although she appeared older than the woman in the photos, the face was Leila's. "Richard's wife is dead."

"You know this Dreamer?" Luke's astonished gaze went from Malachi to Leila.

Leila stared at Malachi, her brows drawn together in confusion. "We've never formally met. I called you here for my son's protection."

"Shut the hell up, lady." Malachi turned back to Luke. "Richard had pictures of her all over his house. Lucien was the only one who kept him going. And now this bitch is impersonating her." He leaned in close to Leila, his nose inches from hers, his face contorted in rage. "How'd you do it, huh? Plastic surgery? What were you hoping to accomplish?" Malachi grabbed her face when she tried to turn away forcing her to look at him. "Answer me."

"I am Leila. Lucien is my son. Richard was my husband." Tears welled up in her eyes. "If you don't listen to me, Lucien is as good as dead."

Malachi was unmoved by her tears. "That's the same thing you said to Stephen at the club. You're the one who tried to kill him." He stepped back, clenched his hands at his side, and imagined his fingers squeezing her throat until the life drained from her. How dare she? He'd watched Richard break down on more than one occasion mourning his dead wife. And she had the nerve to pull this shit? Although he'd never met Leila, he felt like he'd known her. Richard had been a widower for years when Malachi met him, and was still grieving. He'd talked non-stop about Leila and his son. He would not let this freak mock his friend's memory.

"I wasn't there to kill him. I was there to protect him."

Leila jerked her arms and legs against the leather restraints. "You assholes are going to get him killed." The venom in her voice was obvious.

There was no mistake. He could see Lucien in her face. But there was something else.

Malachi jerked around when Luke put a hand on his shoulder then motioned for him to step outside. "You believe her, don't you?"

"It's not possible. She has to be lying." Malachi ran his hands through his hair, pacing the narrow width of the hall. "Damn. Lucien looks just like her." He stopped short, facing Luke. "Where is Lucien?"

"He's downstairs in the training room." Luke leaned against the wall, studying his colleague. "You thinking what I'm thinking?"

Malachi nodded. "How long will a DNA test take?"

Luke stood straight. "A couple of hours. We have Lucien's blood from his physical, and lots of samples from her when she was processed. I'll do the test myself." He slid his finger across the base of his phone. "Dimitri, I need the lab for a couple of hours. No one comes in or out, except me or Malachi, got it?" Luke returned the phone to his pocket. "I don't suppose I need to warn you to keep this under your hat?"

"Of course not." Malachi put his hand on the door knob. "I have quite a few more questions for her though."

Luke started down the hall. "Just keep your cool, and don't trust her for a second. I'll let you know what turns up."

Leila's gaze never left Malachi as he went to sit behind Luke's desk. He poured himself a glass of water and sat back in the chair. "Did you kill Richard?" He tried to sound casual. There was something about her that unnerved him.

Leila just stared dumbly at him for a few seconds. "No. I loved him." She lowered her head, not wanting Malachi to see her tears. "I would have never hurt him. But he died because of me. I faked my death to protect him and the Legacy killed him anyway."

Malachi sat up and clenched his hands in front of him on the table. "Why? Why did they kill him?"

She licked her lips. "Water, please." Malachi poured another glass, impatiently rammed a straw in and held it to her lips.

Leila took a long drink through the straw. She turned her head away when her thirst was quenched. "What do you know about the history of the Catchers?"

Malachi's brows drew together. "We organized because there were a bunch of crazy bitches killing innocent people. We were the only ones capable of stopping you. Whenever nature creates a virus, it also creates a cure." He didn't bother to keep the malice from his voice. "Guess which one you are, sweetheart."

She closed her eyes and leaned her head back. "You've been lied to. Unfortunately, I don't think the people who told you the story knew they were lying. It's been passed down to so many generations, it became fact to the storytellers."

"Yeah right. Got any more good ones?" Malachi sat behind Luke's desk and held his chin in his palm. "I guess I have a little time for a few more fairy tales."

She narrowed her eyes and smiled as if she had some kind of secret he wasn't privy to. "Did Lucien ever tell you his father's ring responded to him before he was of age? Before the age of twenty-one?"

"What's that to you, Dreamer?" His expression became guarded. How in the hell would she know about that?

"No need to try to keep that from me. I've been watching over Lucien since the day Richard died. He used to visit Richard's and my grave every Sunday. I remembered how shocked I was when I saw his dad's ring glowing on his finger." Her forehead creased, straining to remember. "I knew the ring couldn't have been reacting to me. I was too far away. The ring was reacting to him. He has no Dreamer powers, but he has Dreamer blood." She studied Malachi's face, looking for some sign that he believed her. "And so do you. But the Dreamer in your family is so far removed that the ring doesn't react to you. If I am to be true to the way things really are, you are all Dream Protectors."

His face felt hard as stone. "Liar! A Dream Protector? What the hell is that supposed to mean?" He abruptly stood, the chair behind him rolling away and knocking against the wall. "You see, I don't give a damn what label you decide to stamp on us. I just want to know why Lucien has been marked, and what any of this has to do with Richard's murder."

"Someone knew the truth about us. I don't mean the truth about Richard and me. They knew the truth about our history." She took a deep breath. "The Dreamers and The Catchers weren't always enemies. We were meant to be mates."

"Mates?" Malachi laughed. "That's another good one."

"Richard died because he knew the truth. He knew about our history. After I faked my death, I arranged for my great-grandmother's diary to be sent to him. He was supposed to get it to the right people. When he was found dead, I stole the diary back. I refused to risk Lucien's life, but still, he will die because of the truth. He shouldn't exist."

After a deep breath, Leila went on. "You have half of the truth. Dreamers can have only one child, and they are always girls." She pinned Malachi with her glare. "Unless they are with their true mate, a Dream Protector."

Malachi didn't want to hear anymore. It bugged him that she made her story sound so believable. But Dreamers were born liars, and he was getting sick of listening to it. "Why did you want to talk to me in particular? You could have told this little fairy tale to anybody." Frustrated, he crossed to the door. "You know what? Go tell your fairy tale to someone who's got time for bullshit."

Tears welled in her eyes. Her words came out in a rush of desperation. "Why you? Because I knew you and your partner would protect Lucien. When you grabbed Somiar in the club I knew---" She cut her words off and bit her lip.

Malachi froze. "What did you say?"

She seemed absolutely petrified. "You and your partner. I knew you would protect him."

Malachi grabbed a handful of Leila's hair, jerked her head back and studied her for several seconds before he cursed. "Dammit!" How could he miss the resemblance? Something about her face had been bugging him since he walked into the room. He rammed his dreamer pin in Leila's neck, and her body slumped in the chair.

Breathing heavily, he jerked out his phone and dialed Stephen's number. Malachi barely gave him a chance to get his hello out before he spoke. "Stephen, Somiar may be a Dreamer. She could be the one trying to kill Lucien."

Stephen kept his voice conversational. "Well, I'm getting tired. I may just take a nap."

Malachi understood what Stephen met. "No, don't pin her because I'm not one-hundred percent sure. But don't let her out of your sight, understand?

"Got it. See you when you get here."

Malachi dialed Luke. "Listen, I need to get permission to take the Dreamer out of here. And tell Lucien he's got his first assignment. He's coming with me. We've got some Dreamers to catch."

Chapter 13

Somiar didn't like the way Stephen kept looking at her. He would stare when he thought she wasn't aware, then avert his gaze when she glanced his way. "Was that Malachi? Is he coming back yet?"

"Yeah, he just needed to make a couple of stops first." His voice sounded strained, like he was trying to keep control. "He thinks he may have found the Dreamer responsible for an investigation that was never solved a few years back. If he's found her, your life may no longer be in danger."

Somiar's heart pounded so hard she could feel it. She let out a nervous laugh that sounded fake even to her own ears. "That would be a relief. I suppose you know what it's like not knowing whether you'll live another day."

"You have no idea." His statement almost sounded like a contradiction.

Somiar paced the carpet rubbing her temples. She had to get out of this room. Stephen's flinty gaze made her nervous. "I'm going to lie down, all this drama is giving me a headache."

"Suit yourself, doll." Stephen's phone blared. "Wait a minute. That's Mal." Stephen held the phone to his ear for a couple of seconds before speaking to Somiar. "Go ahead and lie down, doll. Mal's going to be a little late and this conversation is private."

114

"Fine." Somiar headed toward her bedroom, then turned. "And Stephen? For the record. I don't appreciate being called 'doll'." Without giving him a chance to answer, she crossed the threshold and slammed the door behind her.

Once in the comfort of her room, she went to her dresser and rummaged through the drawer until her fingers came in contact with the velvet case holding the necklace. She had no feelings of guilt about spying on Stephen. He was such an ass. Somiar placed the necklace around her neck then lay down on the bed. She concentrated on deep breathing and relaxing her body, focusing her thoughts on the balcony. When she felt the cool breeze on her face and the concrete beneath her feet, she opened her eyes. She pressed her body against the wall and again felt an electric charge when she touched the glass. Stephen's voice floated to her.

"Why is she in my apartment? Is she on ice?" He sounded really pissed.

Somiar frowned. She wished she could hear the other end of the conversation.

"Are you sure that was wise? After all, she tried to kill him." A long pause. "She's sleeping in the other room." Somiar could imagine Malachi pacing the floor, hands running through his hair. "The bar? Why not my apartment? I want to see her face."

Somiar's heart hammered in her chest. What if they'd caught Monica? Going to the edge of the balcony, she leaned over as far as she could and studied the balcony below. Closing her eyes, she imagined herself there. Her body became a weightless mass. She opened her eyes when solid ground met her feet. Pressing her body against the wall, she leaned over and peered into the room to see Malachi's retreating back then closed the front door behind him.

She opened the sliding glass door and stepped over the threshold, ignoring the slight shock that again traveled through her body. Every nerve tingled. The hairs on her neck and arms stood on end. Her gaze took in the room. The layout of this apartment wasn't much different from Malachi's, but it was much more personal and inviting. Her feet sank into the plush beige carpet. The colorful paintings on the walls were what she always described as artistic nonsense. They reminded her of a movie she once saw where a monkey painted a picture and it sold for thousands of dollars. There was a plant in almost every corner. The mahogany tables held small stone statues from around the world.

The shiver that crept from base of her spine to the back of her neck made her want to turn and run. All her senses were on high alert. Breathing. Someone was breathing. The soft rhythmic sound led her to the black suede couch.

The woman lying there could be no one but Leila. It was like looking at an older version of herself. Her straight black hair lay over one shoulder, both arms at her side. Slightly parted lips softly inhaled and exhaled, her chest rising and falling with each breath. What the hell was she doing there? Why did they bring her here?

Somiar knelt next to her. She reached out and touched Leila's shoulder gently shaking her, then more vigorously when she got no response. What did they do to her? Was she drugged? Then she saw it. The small star embedded in Leila's neck. The crescent moon engraved in the center reminded her of something.

Her hand went to the pendant at her throat. A crescent moon with a star in the middle. The exact opposite of the pin. She reached out to Leila and closed her fingers around the edges of the pin.

"Hold it right there, Somiar." She froze, her fingers still on the pin at Leila's throat. Stephen's voice was deadly. "Pull that out and you're a dead woman." The click from the hammer of a gun punctuated his sentence.

She remained where she was, sweat beading her forehead. Her heart raced, and though she was sweating, she felt cold as ice. "What's going on here?" she asked without turning. She was afraid if she moved a muscle, he'd blow her brains out.

"Do exactly as I say and I might not kill you. Stand up and turn around, keep your hands where I can see them."

His words were like steel against her back. No doubt, he would shoot her where she stood if she didn't comply. Her hands and legs shook. She stood slowly, hands at shoulder level. Remaining upright was a struggle, but she forced her legs to steady as she slowly turned.

Stephen stared back at her, the large hand gun with a silencer attached aimed at her chest. Next to him was Malachi, his lips stretched to a thin line and hell in his eyes.

"Malachi." His name was a whisper on her lips. She wished the ground would open and swallow her where she stood.

"You want to tell me exactly what you're doing?" He stared at her like he could kill her. When she didn't answer, he clenched his jaw, his hands clenching and unclenching at his thighs. "So, it's true. You're a Dreamer." His gaze never left hers, but his next words were directed at Stephen. "The woman on the couch is her mother. I wasn't sure at first, but look at them."

Stephen's aim never wavered. "You want me to pin her? Nothing would give me greater pleasure." There was no sympathy in his eyes.

"Let me handle this, Stephen." Malachi stalked over to her and seized her wrist. "Stephen just left you upstairs. How did you get past us?"

Somiar licked her dry lips. "I left right after he did. I overheard your conversation and wanted to see who you were talking about." Her desperate gaze darted around the room looking for an escape. His grip on her wrist reminded her of another time. The night she first met him. She fought the tears that burned the back of her eyes. "I figured while you were at the bar I could sneak in here and take a peek at the woman you had."

Stephen took a threatening step toward her. "Liar," he hissed. "We never went to the bar. Malachi met me at the elevator and Lucien took the stairs to the penthouse." He pulled his phone from the case at his waist. "Lucien, did you pass anyone on the stairs?" A short pause. "Check the bedroom and let me know if there's a woman sleeping there."

Somiar cried out as the pressure of Malachi's fingers on her wrist increased. "Malachi, come on. You know who I am. Your ring's not glowing. I can't be a Dreamer." She knew the desperation in her voice unveiled her guilt. There was nothing she wouldn't give right now to make her words true. But how was she to convince him when in her heart she knew she was a fake? "You know who I am."

"Mal, I have confirmation from Lucien. She's still there." Stephen's steely voice came from behind Malachi.

He yanked her closer to him. "I never told you about my ring." His nose was inches from hers, his breath hot on her face. "How are you doing this? How did you get in here? The catcher stones should have kept you out."

"Malachi, listen to me. Don't do this." Tears streamed down her face. The sharp pain in her neck took seconds to register. His face became a blur. Her head spun and her legs went numb.

"Almost ready on this end." Stephen's voice sounded far away, like he was at the other end of a tunnel.

"What did you do to me?"

Malachi's face remained rock hard, but the pain in his eyes was something she would never forget. "Malachi?" Was that a tear sliding down his face? She wanted to brush it from his cheek but her arms were too heavy. "I'm sorry." Trying to fight the darkness overtaking her, Somiar shook her head grabbed his muscled arm for support. Her head lolled to the side. She tried to fight the weight of her own eyelids. It was no use. She collapsed in his arms, allowing the abyss to come.

Chapter 14

"Okay Lucien, pin the body." Stephen's words barely registered as Malachi stood rooted to the spot holding Somiar's body and looking at her face. He brushed her hair back and traced the curve of her mouth. As her body faded from his arms, he tightened his embrace knowing that would not keep her with him.

"How could I have been so blind?" Malachi stared at his hands. Just a few seconds ago the woman he had come to care for deeply had been in his arms. Last night he bared his soul. Had told her things he'd never shared with anyone else. When he made love to her, his body recognized hers. He was more in tune with her than he had ever been with any woman. The way she made him smile this morning, when he walked in on her singing off-key. Her face in the sunlight at The Garden, the wind in her hair. Only a few hours had passed but it seemed so long ago. How could he have been so stupid? He had been a Catcher for seven years. How had he let a pretty face and a good fuck pull the wool over his eyes?

Stephen stuck his phone in his pocket, and twisted the silencer off his gun. "Don't be so hard on yourself, Mal. How were you supposed to know?"

"That crazy story she told me. It didn't make sense. And her name." Malachi collapsed on the soft leather chair. "I should've followed my gut. But after Leila told me about Lucien, it hit me."

Stephen's head jerked up. "Wait. What do you mean after Leila told you about Lucien? Told you what?"

When Malachi didn't answer, Stephen put a firm hand on Malachi's shoulder. "What did she say, Mal?"

"There's a lot you don't know, Stephen. That," he said, pointing a finger at the couch, "is Leila. Richard's Leila, Lucien's mother."

Stephen sat on the heavy mahogany coffee table and rested his arms across his legs. His head cocked to the side. "Come again?"

"You heard me. Somiar is Lucien's sister."

Stephen shook his head in disbelief. "It's not possible. Dreamers can only have one child. A female, and we have her upstairs."

"Or so we thought." Malachi leaned back against the cushions and rubbed his tired eyes. "I didn't believe Leila when she first told the story. But Somiar and Lucien have the same parents. Dreamers can have as many children as they want if they are mated with a Catcher." Malachi let out a heavy sigh. "Lucien and Somiar look just alike. I couldn't figure out where I'd seen her before. I'd seen her face a million times. On Lucien. He's the masculine version of Somiar."

Squeezing his eyes shut, he took a deep breath and tried to force her image from his mind. It wouldn't go away. No matter how hard he tried, her face was there, only now she was laughing at him. Hands gripping the armrests, he forced his anger down deep inside him. Never again would he let anyone get close to him. It never paid.

"How does Lucien feel about helping you catch his mother and sister? I can't imagine him going along with this." He re-holstered his gun and crossed his arms.

"He doesn't know yet. We just got the DNA results. Luke and I thought it best not to tell him right now. He thinks he's on his first assignment." At Stephen's incredulous stare, Malachi stood abruptly. "Don't get all self-righteous on me. It took some time for me to believe it. He might not believe us if we had told him out of the blue."

"That's a cop-out and you know it." Stephen rubbed his fingers over the stubble on his chin. "Do you honestly think that's going to work with Lucien? You should've told him as soon as you found out. He trusted us, and what did you do? You lied to him. This could turn him against us and put him on the side of the Dreamers."

"Lucien's not a Dreamer. According to Mommy Dearest, only females can be Dreamers. Males are Catchers, or Protectors, as she calls us." Malachi turned his back to Stephen. "According to her, we were never meant to be at war."

"Oh really?" Stephen narrowed his eyes. "And the fact that she was willing to kill her own son was an act of peace?"

"She claims she was there to protect him from the real assassin."

"And you believed her?" Stephen headed for the door. "Sorry Mal, but I don't trust any of them."

"Neither do I. Especially Somiar. Not anymore. I see what trusting her cost me." Malachi stalked past Stephen and went out the door. Somiar owed him an explanation, and he damn sure was going to get one from her.

Chapter 15

"If you touch a hair on her head, I'll kill you."

Somiar couldn't place the husky female voice, but it was vaguely familiar. Attempting to focus, she blinked several times and tried to rub her eyes, but couldn't move her arms.

"I don't think you're in any position to be making threats."

Was that Malachi? When her vision cleared, she wished she could fade back into the blackness. It was him leaning over Leila, a smirk marring his handsome face. His flinty gaze slid to her, with what she could only interpret as hatred.

"Well, well, sleeping beauty is awake."

"What happened? What's going on?" Her tongue felt thick in her mouth. She scanned the room, the familiarity of Malachi's penthouse coming into focus. How long had she been out? The black curtains were drawn, so she couldn't get a clue from the sky. A young man sat on the couch, glaring at her. Stephen stood next to her, Leila on the other side bound to a chair. There wasn't a friendly face in the room. Even Leila appeared angry. Somiar stared down at her own restraints, her apprehension growing.

Stephen spoke to the man on the couch. "Lucien, you don't have to stay for this if you don't want to."

Lucien came to stand in front of Leila. "I'm not in the

mood for family reunions but I have questions and I want answers. From both of them."

Leila inhaled sharply, staring at Stephen. "You told him?"

"Yes, *Mother*, they told me." Lucien spat the words out, the disgust in his voice plain. "We had a nice long talk while you were on ice."

"What?" Somiar jerked at her restraints. Her stomach dropped like she was on a roller coaster. "That's impossible. She's not your mother."

"Oh, don't play dumb." Lucien leaned over her, his hand braced on the back of her chair. "Were you in on it with her?"

"In on what?" Somiar twisted in her seat to face Leila. "What's he talking about?"

Lucien straightened and let out a humorless laugh. "Go ahead, Mother Dear. Tell her what I'm talking about."

Somiar didn't like the malice in Lucien's eyes. He really hated her. But why? She had never seen him before in her life. What was all this crazy talk about being Leila's son? The previous night came back to her in waves. The story Malachi had told her. He was talking about her mother. But it couldn't be. One Dreamer, one child. Or was that another one of Monica's lies? What would be the purpose? Why would she lie about something like that? And why would she kill Leila's husband? Nothing made sense.

"Somiar, I'm sorry. I never intended for you to find out about him or me." Leila's eyes glazed over with unshed tears. "I faked my death so the two of you would be safe. I figured if I were out of the picture the two of you, and Richard as well, would be off the Legacy's radar."

Somiar jerked her restraints. "Congratulations, your plan

worked perfectly." Her voice dripped with sarcasm. Not only did she have a father she was never allowed to know, but a brother to boot. "Did we have the same father? Why didn't he raise me?"

Leila licked her lips. "Richard was a Catcher, so I never told him about you. I left him when I found out I was pregnant. I knew you would be a Dreamer and I couldn't bear what would happen when he found out." Leila hung her head. "He had been brought up the way most Catchers had, to hate Dreamers. I found a very nice lady to adopt you, so I knew you'd be safe."

Somiar knew that was a lie. Leila was protecting Monica too. Apparently, she didn't know what a bitch Monica turned out to be. And she wasn't going to bring it up in front of the very men who could use the information against them. They were already in a bad situation. That tidbit certainly wouldn't help. She jerked her head toward Lucien. "So how did he end up in the picture?"

"Richard and I found our way back to each other. I figured since I couldn't have any more kids, that would be the end of it. I could drop out of sight of The Legacy and live a normal life." Her lips stretched to a thin line. "Life has a funny way of being unkind. I found a book that belonged to my great-grandmother in a box of my mother's things. I had read part of it and dismissed it as nonsense. That is, until I found out I was pregnant for the second time."

Lucien paced the floor as Leila told her story. "I don't give a damn about your personal struggles. I only want to know one thing." He squatted between the two women, hands dangling between his legs. "Which one of you bitches were sent to kill me?"

Somiar tore her gaze from Lucien's glare and glanced at Leila, startled at the accusation that flashed in her eyes. "I never tried to kill him. I didn't know anything about him until just now."

"Neither of us tried to kill you." Leila twisted her body toward Stephen. "Okay, both of us were at the club the night of Lucien's party, but neither of us tried to kill him. Who do you think warned you about the attempt on his life?"

Somiar had never been more ashamed of herself. Her lies and half-truths were coming back to bite her in the ass. Her next words came out in a rush. "But I didn't try to kill him. I didn't even know I was a Dreamer then."

Her heart sank at the skeptical twist of his lips. She wished she could go back and change everything. If only she had trusted him with the truth. Maybe he would have understood. Maybe he would have taken her to Leila. Her head snapped up. She remembered hearing Leila's voice that night. The voice in her head. Closing her eyes, she tried to get into Leila's mind. But she could hear nothing but her own jumbled thoughts trying to work through the mess she had created.

"Why should I believe anything you say?" Malachi's words shook with anger.

"Because she's telling the truth." Leila interjected. "Think about that night. Did either of us go anywhere near Lucien? I was the one who warned you his life was in danger. I got a letter the week before. All it said was, 'your son will die on his twenty-first birthday. I hope you're there to watch.' There was no signature. I didn't know who to trust."

Stephen folded his arms. "But someone was after him. If you two were the only Dreamers there, it stands to reason, one of you were there for the job."

Somiar was finding it hard to breathe. "Oh my God." Her words were coming in short gasps. "Get these things off of me." Her arms strained against the leather straps at her wrists. She felt as if the walls were closing in on her, perspiration beading on her forehead.

"What's wrong with her?" Leila's anxiety ridden voice sounded far away.

"Looks like a panic attack." Malachi rushed to unlock Somiar's restraints while Stephen aimed his gun on her. He tilted her face towards his and grabbed her hand putting it to his chest. "Focus, Somiar. Breathe with me."

Somiar gazed into his eyes, her body synchronizing to his. Heartbeat to heartbeat. Breath to breath. In and out. Her head started to clear. This couldn't be happening. How could she be so stupid? She'd played the fool. "Leila, I'm so sorry." Her hand remained on Malachi's chest. Not out of necessity but because even though he hated her, the feel of his heartbeat beneath her palm was somehow reassuring. "We weren't the only Dreamers there that night." She turned to meet Leila's gaze, tears making her vision blurry. "Monica was there too."

Leila stared like someone had slapped her. "No, she couldn't have been. She had no reason to be there. You're mistaken."

Somiar gently placed a trembling hand on top of Leila's. "No, Leila." Her words were shaky. "I'm not."

"Did you actually see her there?"

"No, but I didn't have to. The night after you were captured, Monica told me she was there." Somiar rubbed her upper arms, trying to dispel the goose bumps that had suddenly come up. "She said she'd been watching you for years, and I needed to get you back."

"Unstrap me." Leila jerked against her restraints. "Unstrap me now.

"Oh, you're hilarious," Stephen said, gun in hand. "You have the situation seriously twisted. We ask the questions." He moved behind her and bent over her shoulder, his breath caressing her ear. "And you answer." He ran his fingers through her hair and gave a slight tug. "Now, be a good girl and tell me. Who's Monica?"

"I'm not telling you shit until I'm out of this chair." Somiar admired Leila's ability to sound so controlled. "Besides, where am I going to go? You're the one with the gun."

"She has a point, Stephen. But if she makes one wrong move..." Malachi's expression was hard as stone. "Blow her head off." He went to stand in front of Leila then bent to unlock her restraints.

Somiar gasped. How could he be so callous? Was it so easy for him to order someone's execution? She stared at his profile. She needed to see his eyes. His jaw was clenched, but he did not turn her way.

"Somiar, I need your necklace, and Malachi, I need your computer."

"What? What do you want with my necklace? It was a gift." Somiar clutched the pendant tightly in her palm. She didn't want to part with it. Not even for a moment. It was just one more thing that was being taken from her.

Leila put a reassuring hand on her shoulder. "Please, Somiar, it's important."

Somiar lifted her hands to the clasp when Malachi stopped her. "I don't think so. I want your hands where I can see them at all times." He stood behind her and released the clasp. When his fingers brushed her neck, her eyes fluttered, and she let out a soft sigh.

Malachi held the pendant in his hand and studied it closely. "What the hell...?"

"I was wondering if you'd notice." Leila leaned against the steel breakfast bar that separated the kitchen from the living room. "Weren't you itching to know why your rings didn't react to Somiar?" She looked from Malachi to Stephen. "Come on, don't tell me you forgot that one very important fact."

"Care to clue me in on what she's talking about, Mal?" Stephen stood beside him, peering at the necklace, Lucien in tow. "Is that what I think it is?" Stephen seized the necklace and examined the stone in the center.

"What is it?" Lucien peered over Stephen's shoulder, clearly puzzled. "A ruby moon and an onyx star. Big deal."

Malachi glared at Leila. "This isn't onyx. It's a catcher stone."

Somiar's head jerked up. "Excuse me?"

"It's a catcher stone. Malachi, Steven and Lucien all have one in their rings." Leila surveyed the room. "And if what I've heard is true, they're embedded in the walls of all the Catcher's homes. They're meant to alert you to our presence and keep us out. We can't dream our way in, or walk in while in a dream state."

"I don't understand. This necklace should have been glowing like crazy when she was dreaming. And no way should she have been able to get past any of the doors or windows in Stephen's place, "said Malachi.

"I'm half Catcher." Somiar said in a stunned voice. "Monica said the necklace would only work on me. It's because I'm half Catcher, isn't it? It's also why I was able to get in your apartment." She raised her head, her eyes searching for affirmation from Leila.

Leila nodded, then held her hand out to Malachi. "The necklace please. There's something I need to show all of you." She took the necklace and studied the clasp. Pressing tightly on a notch in the clasp with one thumb, she slid the black star to the tip of the crescent moon with the other and extracted a tiny computer chip. "It's a copy of my grandmother's diary."

Holstering his gun, Stephen took the chip from her and downloaded it onto Malachi's computer. "There are over four hundred pages here."

"Yeah, and that's just my great-grandmother's story. I figured that was the most important stuff. It tells how she found out about the true cause of the war between us and what someone like Somiar and Lucien can do."

"What do you mean someone like us?" Lucien folded his arms in front of him. "What exactly can we do?"

"Well, you already know your stones don't work on Somiar as long as she has a stone on her, but what you don't know is Lucien doesn't need a ring to detect a Dreamer. The ringing in your ears would still happen whether you wore your ring or not." Leila gave a little laugh at Lucien's disappointed expression. "Believe it or not, that's a pretty good feat. We know to watch out for those rings. A Dreamer would never see you coming. Plus, you can heal Dreamers and Catchers."

"Yeah, so can a doctor." Lucien's sarcasm clearly irritated Leila.

She pursed her lips and narrowed her eyes. "And for the record, I hate a smart ass."

Lucien glared at her. "And I don't give a shit. Don't try to play mommy now. You gave up all rights the moment you left me." He turned from her and stalked to the other side of the room, reminding Somiar of a petulant child.

The pain in Leila's eyes made Somiar almost feel sorry for her. Almost. She wasn't ready to let her completely off the hook. If it hadn't been for her, none of them would be in this mess. All her life she'd dreamed of a mother who would hold her close and tell her everything was going to be all right. If at this moment, Leila opened her arms to her daughter, she didn't know if she could resist running into them and not letting go. But none of those things happened. What she got was a woman who abandoned her for a man.

Lucien had some nerve. At least he had known one of his parents. A father who loved him. She'd been robbed of everything, her dreams were only a fairy tale, with no happily-ever-after.

Leila stretched out her arm and dug her fingernails into her flesh, dragging them downward, drawing blood.

"Are you crazy?" Malachi snatched her hand away from her arm. "What are you trying to do?"

Leila narrowed her eyes. "Were you willing to let me use a knife?" She jerked her head at Stephen. "Or maybe your friend would have been nice enough to let me borrow his gun."

Malachi ignored her sarcasm. "I've got some disinfectant in the bathroom. We need to get those gashes cleaned."

"Weren't you listening to a word I said?" Leila snatched her arm away from him. She moved to Lucien's side and took his hand in hers. He resisted, but she kept a firm grip.

In a lightning fast move, Stephen drew his gun back out of his holster and aimed for Leila's head. "Let him go. Your ass depends on it."

"No!" Somiar jumped to her feet. Malachi was instantly behind her, his arms around her in an imprisoning embrace.

"She only dies if she gives him a reason." There was a slight catch in Malachi's voice that made Somiar want to trust him. She prayed he wouldn't let anything happen to Leila. She sagged against him, not sure how much more she could take.

"I would never hurt you, Lucien. I know you don't want to, nor do you have a reason, but please listen to me just this once," Leila pleaded.

Lucien held his other hand up at Malachi and Stephen. "She's not hurting me, and I don't see a weapon. Let's hear her out."

Never taking her gaze from his, she placed his hand over her bleeding arm. "Close your eyes."

Lucien glanced uneasily at Malachi and Stephen. "Keep an eye on her guys." At their brief nod, he did what she asked.

Leila kept her hand over Lucien's. "Concentrate. Imagine you can hear your own heartbeat. With each beat, the scars fade more and more."

Lucien's eyelids jumped rapidly, in REM sleep. His breathing became slow and deep. With a grunt his eyes flew open. He glanced down to where his hand covered Leila's arm, winced and snatched his hand away. "What the hell was that?" Lucien held his hand up in front of his face inspecting his palms. "My hand is burning."

"So is my arm, but it'll only last a couple of minutes." Leila blew on her arm. Her wounds were gone. "Man, when my great-grandmother wrote that stinging and burning was a side effect, she wasn't just whistling Dixie."

Malachi returned his attention to the computer screen. His grip on Somiar loosened, but he never took his arms from around her. "You mean that's in there? If Catchers can heal each other, why can't Stephen and I do it?"

Leila took a seat on the black leather couch. "Because your mothers weren't Dreamers. The males and females of our race had abilities that were meant to compliment each other. The war changed everything. Our abilities are no longer in harmony." She bit her lip. "Where do you think Dreamers and Catchers come from?"

"Seriously?" Stephen chuckled. "Didn't your parents have that talk with you when you were a kid?"

Leila shot Stephen an irritated glare. "Very funny. But believe me, what I'm about to tell you is not going to go down well."

"Oh, this sounds serious." Stephen sat on the chair across from her and placed his gun on the table, the mocking smile never leaving his face.

"The only reason you have the power of a Catcher is because you are the descendant of a Dreamer. The only reason Dreamers exist is because somewhere there's a Catcher in our family tree. We are all connected. Our ancestors all come from the same race of people. The women have one set of gifts, and

the men, another. Now stick that in your pipe and smoke it."
Leila sat back, a mocking smile now on her face.

She turned her attention to Malachi still holding Somiar in
a loose embrace. "But there's still one thing you're able to do,
whether your mothers were Dreamers or not. You still know
your mate when you find her." Leila went to stand in front of
Malachi and Somiar. "The male sees his mate in visions."

Malachi's arms went limp at his sides. He stepped back
from Somiar as if her touch burned him.

"What?" Somiar turned to face him. "What's wrong with
you?"

"The first night you were here. When I took you to your
room. I saw the two of us." Malachi turned to face Leila. "Is
that in there too?"

"No." Leila put a reassuring hand on Somiar's arm, but
Somiar shrugged it off. "Like I said, this is only one of the
books."

Malachi turned his back to her. "Where's the rest?"

"I buried them." Leila gave a sigh of relief when Stephen re-
holstered his gun. "They're in my grave in a metal box. About
halfway down."

Chapter 16

Somiar fought against the thick, inky blackness that embraced her. It was warm and comforting, offering peace of mind. Surrender would be so easy. It promised rest. No thoughts, no dreams, no worries. But she would not be lulled into a false sense of security. And she would not let others decide when she would face her life.

The dark mist started to lift, as if someone were removing blinders from her eyes. When her vision cleared, she recognized the room she was standing in. It was Malachi's guest room. She gazed at her unconscious body lying on the bed. She appeared peaceful in her blue plaid pajama pants and t-shirt, the hated star-shaped pin stuck in her neck. Her lips stretched into a slow smile. Apparently, the catcher stones weren't the only one of their toys that didn't work on her.

Somiar reached for the pin on her body, then decided to leave it where it was. If Malachi checked on her and the pin was gone, he would think she was trying to escape.

Although they had all come to an understanding, she and Leila were still not fully trusted by Malachi and Stephen. After an animated conversation over a cold dinner about her great-grandmother's diary, it was agreed that Somiar and Leila would stay apart and on ice for the night.

Somiar stayed in Malachi's guest room and Leila stayed

in Stephen's. Lucien's accommodations were not disclosed to the women.

What she wanted right now, more than anything else was to be alone with her thoughts. Away from everyone. She closed her eyes and imagined Monica's property in Jamaica. When her bare feet made contact with the soft, green grass, she opened her eyes. Stepping to the edge of the cliff, Somiar gazed out at the private beach below. The white silk sarong she had dressed herself in fluttered in the breeze and caressed her body.

White sand glistened in the moonlight, undisturbed except for the water that gently lapped the shore. An occasional spray sprung up from the boulders on the left side of the beach. She smiled when she turned to see the fireflies twinkle around the white marble statues in the garden behind her. Millions of stars dotted the sky. They weren't as vivid in Atlanta. The city was too bright and noisy. All the money in the world couldn't buy the beauty and tranquility of a Jamaican night.

The main house was too far away to be seen from here and the house staff was never there if no one was in residence. The caretaker came by twice a week to take care of the property, but she was sure he was at home with his family at this hour. After all, Jamaica was only an hour behind Atlanta.

Sitting down on one of the white wooden recliners, she drew her knees up to her chest, rested her chin on them and sighed heavily. Why couldn't she and Malachi have met under normal circumstances? After all they'd been through, what kind of life together could they possibly have? Their whole relationship was built on lies, manipulation and half-truths.

And most of it was on her part. She wanted him to see the real her. Problem was she wasn't sure what the real her was. In a matter of days, she had been pulled, twisted and turned more than salt water taffy.

She thought she knew who she was, but that turned out to be one big farce. What was she supposed to do now? What did people do when they found out everything they thought they knew about themselves was bullshit?

When she was with Malachi all the craziness faded, at least for a little while. If only he were with her now. There was nothing she wouldn't give to see him strolling down the path.

At first, she thought she imagined the movement off to her right side. She turned her head and gasped, springing to her feet at the sight of a large man striding up the beach toward her. Her heart beat faster as he got closer, and she could make out features. Malachi. The white, short sleeved shirt he wore was open down the front and showed off his incredibly muscular chest and washboard stomach. His jeans hung low on his hips, hugging his thighs. Where there was no grass, his bare feet kicked up small clouds of sand.

She wanted to turn and run, but her feet were rooted to the spot. Nothing was making sense. She'd only been there few minutes. There was no way he could have known where she was. Her body was still in his guest room, and she hadn't sensed anyone trying to wake her. Her brows drew together when she noticed he wasn't wearing his ring. What the hell was going on?

Without a word he snaked one arm around her waist, then lifted the other to brush her cheek with the back of his hand.

His head came toward her, and he brushed her lips with a feather soft kiss.

She didn't move, convinced her imagination was playing tricks on her. If she moved, he would disappear. And she didn't want him to go. "How did you get here?" She whispered the words against his mouth.

He withdrew his kips and replaced them with a finger. "No questions. This is my dream and I want things my way." His hand slid up her arm to her shoulder and unhooked the diamond and pearl clasp holding her sarong closed.

She caught the soft material before it could fall, using it to shield the front of her body from his heated gaze. She shivered slightly but the warm tropical breeze brushing across her bare ass had nothing to do with it. Oh, dear Lord, he thought he was dreaming. But he was a Catcher. He shouldn't be here. Even if he were half Dreamer, he wouldn't be able to project.

And yet... her blood ran cold as she remembered her last thought. She wanted him here with her. With a jolt she realized he hadn't projected himself to her side. She'd pulled him in. He was here because of her. Oh, great. Now she was in a real-life version of "Nightmare on Elm Street."

She needed to study that damned book and find out exactly what she was capable of. Stumbling on her abilities was turning out to be more than a little annoying. He would think she did this on purpose. Trying to ignore her pounding heart, she turned her head when he moved to kiss her again. She had to stop him. "Malachi, listen to me. This isn't'-----"

He cut her off with his mouth on hers. There was nothing tender about this kiss. It was full of passion and fire. His tongue delved into her mouth, tasting and exploring. He plunged his fingers in her hair and gently tugged her head back to run his lips and tongue down her neck. Wrapping his fingers around her slim hands still full of the silk that hid her body, he nudged them down to her waist. When his lips closed around her nipple, Somiar inhaled sharply.

She thought her legs would buckle under her, but Malachi held her steady in his arms. The feel of her body entangled with his consumed her. All thoughts of warning him flew from her mind. The primitive part of her took over. She wanted to take him. And she wanted to take him slowly.

She pulled away from him, letting the sarong slide through her fingers, forming a shimmering white pool at her feet. When he reached for her, she stepped back. "No." The word almost sounded like a hiss.

"No?"

"Have you ever let a woman take charge, Malachi?" Somiar smiled when he shook his head. "Let me. Let me have this night my way. You won't regret it." She moved in again, close, not letting their bodies touch, and ran a finger down his chest to the waistband of his jeans. "Let me take what I want."

The moonlight showed his physique to perfection. Light and shadow played across his muscled body at the whims of the clouds in the sky. Had it not been for the rise and fall of his chest, he could have been mistaken for one of the garden statues. "As you wish."

Somiar slid his shirt down his arms and let it fall to the grass. She buried her face in his chest, taking in the masculine scent of him. Her nails slid down his back as her tongue made its way down his body. When she came to the top of his jeans, she was pleasantly surprised at how easy it was to release the button. Gently swirling her tongue around his navel, she yanked the stiff denim down his thighs past his knees. He lifted his legs out one at a time and kicked them aside.

Resting her knees in the grass, she drew his dick into her mouth and reveled in the feel of him at the back of her throat. She pulled back far enough to notice his fingers clenching and unclenching at his sides. Covering his hands with hers, she led them to both sides of her head and let him guide her motions. He was almost out of control and she could tell. She wrapped her fingers around the base of his dick to keep it from gagging her as he slammed himself into her mouth. When she felt his body tense, she pulled back and stood.

Before he could speak, she pressed her lips to his, and let her tongue explore his mouth. The slick feel of his teeth, the ridges at the roof of his mouth, and the texture of his tongue spurred her on. His hands ran down her back and squeezed her ass. Putting slight pressure on his shoulders, she urged him to his knees.

Somiar almost tipped over when he buried his face in her pussy. There wasn't a spot his tongue didn't reach. When she knew she was on the edge of a climax, she put her hands on the sides of his face, gently tilting it up, so she could gaze into his eyes.

Denying her own release, she joined him, kneeling in the grass. "Lay back, baby."

He reclined slowly, abs rippling with every movement. Somiar straddled him and, never taking her eyes from his, impaled herself on him. She entwined her fingers with his and pressed his hands into the grass. "Don't close your eyes, Malachi. I want to watch you come, and I want you to watch me." She lifted her body until the tip of his dick was the only part inside her and slammed herself back down. His body tensed and his teeth clenched. "Not yet, Malachi."

At first, she rode him slow and steady then faster as she felt her own climax build. His hands closed tighter and tighter around hers until she thought her fingers would break. His excitement only added to hers.

"Now, Malachi." Her heart galloped in her chest, and her head was spinning. With great effort she managed to keep her eyes locked on his.

He exhaled loudly and grabbed her ass, rising up to meet her. Every muscle in his body tensed and his dick pulsed inside her.

Somiar collapsed against his chest, attempting to even her breathing. This was what she needed. Tomorrow would take care of itself. Right now, hearing his erratic heartbeat drum in her ear, his fingers running through her hair and down her back was enough.

"I love being with you." Malachi's deep voice vibrated against her cheek, making her smile.

"I love being with you too, baby." Oh, if only she could tell him. If only what she was, and what he was, didn't matter. So what if Leila thought they were destined to be together? The choice was ultimately theirs.

"Can I only have you like this in my dreams?" The rumble in his chest from his deep voice vibrated against her ear.

She wanted to revel in the sensation but something was wrong. Something was very wrong. The hairs on the back of her neck stood on end, and a familiar tingle snaked its way down her spine. It was something she experienced only one time before while in a dream state. Oh, God, please no. Don't let it be...

"Of course, you idiot." Monica's voice rang out from behind them.

They jumped to their feet at the intrusion. Somiar snatched up her sarong and stepped in front of Malachi in a protective stance. Why couldn't Monica give them just one night? The anger in her threatened to boil over. How dare she? "Stay away from him, Monica. Stay away from us, or I swear I'll kill you."

Monica threw her head back and gave a hearty laugh. "Please. Do you really think you could take me on?"

Malachi stepped in front of Somiar, his hastily donned jeans still unbuttoned. "Okay. This is my dream and I'm not amused. I want things back to the way they were before."

"Baby, you don't understand." She looked past him and saw Monica pull the dagger front the sheath strapped to her arm. "I need to get you out of here. You're not dreaming."

The lack of interest in Malachi's eyes was terrifying. He didn't believe her. She had to wake him up. "I won't let you hurt him, Monica." Darting around him, she slammed both of her hands into his back and pushed him with all her might until he stumbled over the cliff.

She stepped to the edge and peered over, relieved to see her plan had worked. His body was nowhere in sight.

"Really, Somiar, I don't have a problem with you sleeping with the enemy if it helps get what you want, but you weren't supposed to save his life." Monica returned her dagger to its sheath.

"And what about Leila's life?" Somiar's lip curled in revulsion. "Was I really supposed to save her, or was I supposed to deliver her to you?" Somiar backed away from Monica. "Despite what you may think, I'm not stupid. Did you really think I wouldn't figure it out? You killed her husband. You knew that when she found out, there was no way she was going to let you live."

"Who have you been talking to?" Monica stalked toward her like a predator after its prey. "Is Leila with you?"

Somiar shot a wicked grin at Monica. "Don't know, do you?" She turned and sprinted to the cliff, leaping off the edge.

Chapter 17

Malachi jerked upright from the mattress covered in sweat. He hated those dreams of falling from high places. But something about this one nagged him. Something besides the fact that after making love to him, Somiar pushed him off a cliff. He wasn't sure how to interpret that one. Wasn't sure he even wanted to. It would be a big blow to his ego to imagine she thought he was a lousy lay.

There was something she'd said. He tried to remember everything, but it wouldn't come to him. He threw the sheet back and went to take a shower. Stephen wouldn't be up for hours, and he knew he wouldn't be able to go back to sleep.

Lukewarm showers always had a way of making him ready to face the day. The massage setting on his shower head got his blood pumping and cleared the cobwebs from the night before. He closed his eyes and enjoyed the feel of the warm water cascading over him. Bits and pieces of his dream flashed through his mind. Somiar standing in front of him. You're not dreaming. He could almost hear her voice. He could see her as plain as day. Stay away from him, Monica.

Monica! Malachi's eyes snapped open. He turned the water off and snatched his robe from the hook outside the shower door. Monica had come up in their conversation earlier in the evening but everyone was so caught up in the events of the night, no one had thought to follow up on her. What if that was the plan? Maybe Leila and Somiar didn't want any questions about Monica.

He stopped short when he stepped over the threshold. Somiar was sitting on the corner of his bed, staring at the dreamer pin in her hand.

"I tried to tell you it wasn't a dream, but you wouldn't listen." She looked up at him with empty eyes.

"Who released you?" he scanned the room. Keeping his back to the wall, he inched toward his dresser, hoping to get to his gun before whoever her accomplice was attacked him.

"This pin doesn't work on me." Somiar placed the pin on the bedside table next to her.

"It was real? You mean we actually...?"

Somiar nodded. "Yes, we did. And yes, Monica was real too. She knows everything, Malachi. She knows we have Leila, and that I know what she's up to."

"You warned her?" Malachi stepped further into the room. Surely, she couldn't be so cold. She wouldn't make love to him and betray him a few minutes later. But she did push him off a cliff.

"I never warned her about anything. She was the one who sent me to you. Told me my birth mother was in trouble and the Catchers would interrogate, then kill her. She said I was supposed to save Leila." Somiar looked up, eyes shining with unshed tears. "It was all a lie. After I got Leila, Monica intended to kill her. She was going to kill my mother and had no qualms with using me," Somiar pressed her palm against her chest and sniffed, "to help her do it." An almost hysterical laugh escaped her lips. "I'd seen those damned black roses in her study a thousand times."

Malachi's spine stiffened when Somiar mentioned black roses. She knew who the Black Rose was? So much was starting to make sense. The fact that Somiar was still alive had nothing to do with his ability to guard her. Rose didn't want her dead. Were they working together?

Her lips twitched, like she was trying to keep her emotions in check. Tears streamed down her face and Somiar angrily wiped them away. She dropped her hand and let her head hang. Her shoulders drooped in defeat, her body rocking back and forth. "Monica was the only mother I'd ever known, and she was going to take everything from me. My father is gone because of her, but she didn't stop there. My real mother had to go, and a brother I didn't even know I had. I would have no one left, but she didn't care." Somiar sniffed and let out a short, humorless laugh. "You know, I never even had her. I was always treated as an afterthought. She fed me and kept a roof over my head. But she did that for our pet dogs too."

Rising, tears coursing down her face, she said, "If I hadn't shocked you into waking up, she would have killed you too." She wrapped her arms around her stomach. "Why doesn't she love me, Malachi? What did I ever do to her? I didn't ask to be here." Her voice shook uncontrollably. "Why would she do that? Why does she hate me?"

Malachi put his arms around her, holding her close, stroking her hair as she kept asking, "Why, why?" She kept her face pressed to his chest, holding onto the lapels of his bathrobe like her life depended on it.

What had that crazy bitch done to her? He picked her up

and sat on the bed with her in his lap rocking her back and forth. "She won't hurt anyone else." Somiar's tears made him hurt for her, but the defeat he saw in her face scared him. She was ready to give up. "It's going to be okay, sweetheart. We're not going to let anything happen to Leila or Lucien."

He would hold her as long as she needed him to. He placed a gentle fingertip to her chin and titled her head up toward him. "Or you. I promise."

She reached up and curled an arm around his neck, and pressed her lips to his. Her kiss started slow and sweet, then got more demanding.

It took everything in him to pull back. "No, baby. That's not going to make this go away." He stood with her still in his arms, and then lowered her to his bed. "I'm going to wake the others up. You'll be okay until I get back?"

Somiar nodded and curled up into a ball. "I'll be fine."
***

Stephen answered the banging on his door, nine-millimeter complete with silencer in hand.

Malachi frowned at the barrel pointed at his forehead. "Why the hell are you answering your door with a gun?"

"Oh, I don't know. The fact that we have two Dreamers plus baby boy with us isn't a good reason?" Stephen tapped his finger against his chin. "What else could there be?"

"Can the sarcasm. We have a problem." Malachi stalked past Stephen. "Don't freak out but I met The Black Rose tonight. In her actual body."

"What? Where? How'd you know it was her? And what the hell are you thinking to leave a Dreamer in your place unguarded?"

"Don't get your drawers in a bunch. What's she going to do? Steal my blender?"

"Well as long as you have her on ice, I guess there's no harm."

"Our dreamer pins don't work on Somiar. If she wanted me dead, it'd be a done deal by now. She was dreaming and apparently pulled me to her while I was asleep. I wasn't even aware it wasn't a dream until a few minutes ago." Malachi plopped down on Stephens's leather couch, and propped a foot on the table.

"You mind closing your legs, Mal? That bathrobe doesn't cover much and I don't want to know you that well."

"Sorry." Malachi went to Stephen's desk and opened his laptop. "You still got the information on Somiar stored in here?"

"Sure. But none of the freaky shit we found out tonight is in there. If you go by her info, she's a perfectly normal person. Matter-of-fact, it makes her seem downright boring."

"No, I don't think so." Malachi skimmed her file until he found the name he was looking for. Monica Ayers. He clicked on her name and held his breath while he waited for her picture to come up. He sat back and sighed, running a hand over his face when the woman from his "dream" popped up on the monitor. "Stephen, let me introduce you to The Black Rose."

Stephen peered at the woman on the screen. "But that's Somiar's adoptive mother. You mean we've been getting our asses handed to us by an old woman?"

"Yeah, and I was hoping it wouldn't be. But Somiar said she's seen black roses in her mother's study a thousand times.

And there is no question." Malachi motioned at the screen. "This is the woman I saw tonight."

Stephen pulled his phone from his robe pocket and hit a button. "Luke. We're going to need some Catchers on West Paces Ferry in Buckhead. I'll text you the address. And keep it on the low. Jared is having enough trouble keeping the police off our asses."

Malachi held a hand out. "Give me the phone, Stephen." He pressed the receiver to his ear and navigated the mouse to the computer with his other hand. "Hey, Luke, Mal here. I need you to do an extensive search on Monica Ayers. I think she may be Rose. Even if it takes hacking into her medical records and computer files. If this lady takes a shit, I want to know about it." Without giving Luke a chance to answer, he handed the phone back to Stephen.

"Yeah, I'm texting the address now." Stephen disconnected the call. His fingers flew over the phone's keyboard then he tucked it back in his pocket. "Where's Somiar?"

"I told you I left her upstairs."

"Are you out of your mind? Just because she says something is so doesn't make it true. I've seen the way you look at her. You're thinking with your dick and that's not like you."

"Fuck you, Stephen."

"Not in your wildest dreams. Go keep an eye on her. I'll be up in a minute with Leila and Lucien."

Malachi bit back a sarcastic retort and left. He wasn't a man who took kindly to being talked down to, but this was not the time for him to get into it with Stephen. There was too much to do. This was the closest they'd ever come to catching Rose. He'd beat the shit out of Stephen later. Right now, he had to make sure Somiar was okay.

***

Somiar's head pounded. What had happened in the last few days, was too much to take in. So long as she didn't have to see Monica, she didn't have to deal with the truth. But the moment she saw her face on that cliff, it became real. Monica didn't give a damn about her or Leila. After she killed Leila, maybe Somiar would be next.

The bedroom door swung open. "Somiar?" Malachi stepped inside, and she felt the mattress sink when he sat down next to her. "Everyone will be here in a few minutes."

This was her life now. Waiting for the Scooby gang to show up and fight the bad guys. Learning in increments who and what she was from the pages of a book. Forgetting everything she thought she knew about herself. Most people have their whole lives to discover who they are. She had days. And she didn't want any of it. She didn't want to make love in paradise with a man who didn't know she was real. Didn't want to have to watch for things that go bump in the night. One normal moment. It was all she wanted. Normalcy. What a beautiful lie. And she hoped he would give it to her. "Hold me, Malachi? Just for a minute?"

She sighed when he snuggled up behind her, arms encircling her in a protective embrace. His breath was warm and reassuring on the top of her head. She wanted to sink deep inside him and stay there.

The voices in the other room shattered all illusions of hiding there with him forever. "I guess Stephen decided to let himself in." Malachi rose from the bed and brushed her hair

back. "You go ahead and get yourself together. They can wait."
He threw on a pair of jeans and a t-shirt before leaving the
room.

Somiar sat up and gave a weak smile. "I'll be right there."
Her pity party was over. It was time to face her life.

Chapter 18

Somiar entered the room and surveyed the faces of the people who held her life in their hands. And she held their lives in hers. All of them strangers, but connected. There was pity on Stephens face, and dislike on Lucien's. Guilt and shame practically oozed from Leila. Somiar stared at Leila, wanting her to look back. To see her. She waited for what seemed like hours for Leila to meet her gaze, but Leila wouldn't even look in her direction.

Malachi was the only one whose face registered compassion and concern. "We have to come up with a plan. Monica knows Somiar is with us. We have to figure out what she wants from her."

Somiar looked at Leila with disdain. "She wants you."

"Me?" Leila was taken aback. "Why me?"

"Why don't you tell us? The only reason I got into this mess was because she wanted me to rescue you." Somiar leaned against the wall and folded her arms. The time had come. It was time for all of them to lay their cards on the table. This whole mess started with Leila, so it was only fair that Leila started the process of fixing it.

"But that's ridiculous. Once a Dreamer is captured, we don't try to get her back. It's too risky. We'd have Catchers all over us straightaway. We know from the beginning, not to expect help. Why would Monica do that?" Leila drew her brows together gazing at Somiar as if the answer to her question was written on her face. "And sending someone as green as you makes absolutely no sense."

"She gave me the necklace and told me how it works. She knows what I am." Somiar sneered.

"No." Leila shook her head. "All I told her was to give you the necklace. I never told her about your father. I knew she wouldn't understand. When Richard died, I vowed..."

"She killed him." Somiar's hands sliced through the air, her voice rising until she was shouting. "You don't get it, do you? She's a liar. She killed my father because he was a Catcher. The fact that he was your husband, or that Lucien is your son doesn't matter to her. Did you think any of us matter?" "Somiar turned her back to Leila, and lowered her voice. "Did you think I matter?"

Malachi came up behind her and took her in his arms. She was grateful for the comfort of his embrace. To know that at that moment she did matter, at least to him. And he didn't care who saw it.

"I thought I was so careful." Leila's words were full of sorrow, but Somiar couldn't bring herself to let them touch her.

One mother had betrayed her mightily. This one would not be given that same chance. "Oh, spare me the self-pity. You tricked her into raising the daughter of her worst enemies. Did you expect her to thank you?"

Leila bolted from her seat and ran into the bathroom. She flung open cabinet doors and pulled out drawers, rummaging through their contents and tossing them aside.

"What the hell are you doing?" Malachi was the first to reach her.

"Where are your tranquilizers?" Leila pulled more bottles and packages from the cabinets and paused at a bottle of cough syrup. "I'm going after her. I won't let her get away with this."

Somiar stood rooted to the spot, stunned as she looked past Malachi and watched her mother scan the ingredients.

Leila popped the top and raised her hand to drink directly from the container.

Malachi grabbed the bottle before she could accomplish her goal. The red syrup splashed out of the bottle and splattered all over the spotless white sink. "You're not going after anybody." He guided her back to the living room. "There's no way we're going to let you go anywhere half-cocked. You'll only get yourself or maybe one of us killed." He turned to Stephen. "Make sure you pin her tonight."

At Leila's indignant gasp, he cast her rueful smile. "It's for your own good."

She jerked away from him. "You got a better plan?"

"As a matter of fact, I do. Both Somiar and Lucien need to be trained. Stephen and I can take care of the weapons training. And you can take care of the hand-to-hand fighting." He turned to Somiar. "Do you have any hand-to-hand training, or experience with any kind of weapons?"

Somiar ran a hand over her tired eyes. She regretted that his arms were no longer around her, consoling her. It was back to business. "Martial arts training since I was five. My instructor also trained me in the use of a sai and sword fighting. Monica insisted I learn."

"You're just a regular menace to society, aren't you?" Lucien's tone was full of venom.

"I liked you better when you sat there like a mute." Somiar was sick and tired of Lucien's shit. She didn't like him any more than he liked her, and she didn't care if he knew it.

"Fuck you, bitch." Lucien rose from the couch and headed for the door.

Before he could pass, Malachi grabbed him by his shirt and rammed his back against the wall. "Watch your mouth, boy. The next time you talk to her that way, you'll be drinking your meals through a straw."

Lucien gave him an icy stare. "Nice to know where you stand, brother."

Somiar had to hand it to Lucien. He had guts. The one time Malachi had given her that look was when he caught her trying to rescue Leila. It was enough to almost make her collapse.

"I stand with you both." Malachi released Lucien's shirt. "And I won't let this destroy either of you."

Eminem's "Not Afraid" blasted from the vicinity of Stephen's waist. He pulled his cell phone from its clip. "Whatcha got, Luke?" After listening a few minutes, he spoke again. "I thought so. Keep a small detail of Watchers there anyway." Pause. "Yes, around the clock."

Returning the phone to its case, he grimaced. "Black Rose's house is empty. Furniture's covered, and the servants are gone."

"Oh, this is perfect." Lucien glared at Leila. "Why couldn't you have just stayed away? I was happier when I thought you were dead."

Unchecked tears spilled from Leila's eyes. She wrapped her arms around her waist and turned from the others. Head bowed, she went to stand at the end of the couch next to the fireplace.

Somiar was surprised when Stephen placed a comforting hand on Leila's shoulder. She had started to think the man was made of stone. It was the first compassionate thing she'd seen him do.

"Lucien, enough." Malachi's voice rang out across the room. "It's time to grow up. No one likes this situation, but here it is. Now we have to deal with it."

"I'm going to bed." Lucien yanked open the front door. "Thanks everybody for turning my life to shit."

After he left, the silence in the room was deafening. Stephen clapped and rubbed his hands together. "Well, that was awkward." The compassionate man that had been there before had vanished. The smart ass was back.

Somiar moved to the couch and flopped on the cushions, sitting as far from Leila as possible. She didn't want her close right now. She eyed the stranger who had given her life, then walked out of it. But she was no longer a child. She was a grown woman, and a survivor. She no longer needed a mother. Leila had brought her nothing but grief. All she wanted was an end to this nightmare. When it was over, Leila would go back to meaning what she had before. Nothing.

So why did she still feel the urge to go to her? To put her head on her mother's chest and let herself be hugged.

Malachi cleared his throat. "Stephen, take Leila to her room and pin her. We all need a good night's sleep. And make sure Lucien's okay."

Stephen raised his hand in a mock salute. "You got it." He turned to Leila, his voice gentle. "Come on, Lee. Time for bed."

Leila raised her head, all of her sorrow and anguish on her face. Her eyes were red, the lids puffy. "I've lost him, haven't I? My own son wishes I were dead."

"He's just a kid, Lee. It's a lot to handle in one day. He was just lashing out." Stephen turned her toward the door.

Leila's steps were mechanical. She didn't seem to know where she was going and didn't care. There was a part of Somiar that wanted to run to her and tell her everything was going to be okay. But another cruel part whispered in the back of her mind. Where was she when you needed her?

After everyone else had gone, Somiar was unsure what to do next. What had happened between them in Jamaica was the elephant in the room. Instead of doing nothing, she traced the seam on the leather couch with her fingers.

"Somiar. We need to get some rest. I'll see you in the morning."

She looked up in time to see his retreating back. "Malachi." His name escaped her lips before she could stop it.

He turned to her, a question in his eyes. "What's wrong?"

"I don't want to be alone tonight."

"You don't have to be. I'll sit out here with you." He moved to sit next to her on the couch.

"No." Her lips brushed his. "I want to stay in there." She inclined her head toward his room. "With you."

Malachi pulled away. "Somiar, stop. You're trying to bury your grief and this isn't the way to do it."

"I know what I'm doing. If you don't want me, just say

so." Somiar left the couch and turned toward her room. He couldn't get past what she was. What she had no control over. A Dreamer. "I understand." There it was. Her feet felt like they had lead weights on them, tugging mercilessly at her with each step. She was so tired. Tired of the games, the madness.

She didn't want to face the night alone. In her mind, Monica would be in every corner, lurking behind every curtain. Her gaze went from the bed to the overstuffed chair in her room. Maybe if she sat there, she could stay awake. If she could rest without closing her eyes, the loneliness, the emptiness of the night wouldn't consume her. Her body screamed for Malachi. But it wasn't to be. He didn't want her.

"Somiar." Malachi's voice was soft and deep behind her. He was so close she could feel his heat against her back. His strong hands touched her shoulders.

She wanted to turn, press her face against his chest, inhale his male scent. But she couldn't take the chance. She would die if he denied her again.

"I feel you." His arms went around her waist, and she leaned back against him. "Your body calls for me, Somiar. And mine wants you." He turned to face her and lifted her in his arms. He carried her to his room and laid her on his bed. His lips touched hers in a soft, gentle kiss. The feel of his tongue teasing and tasting her mouth made Gooseflesh rise on her arms. This wasn't like the last time. There was no rush, no demanding urgency, just slow exploration.

His hands slid up her shirt, palms down, taking the material with them. The feel of his palms against her skin made her shudder. She raised her arms and arched her back as he pulled the material over her head. Returning the favor, she tugged off his shirt, playing with the soft curls on his chest. Her hands glided down his stomach to unfasten his jeans while her tongue teased his nipples. His hand followed hers and he unzipped himself. No underwear. She liked that.

She lifted her hips, so he could slide her pajama bottoms off. He claimed her lips with a kiss that left her breathless. His thumbs brushed across her hardened nipples, while his thigh rubbed against her wet pussy. She moaned into his mouth. "Take me Malachi, please. Now."

"No. This will not be rushed. I want you to feel me like I feel you." He held her tight against him, his warm breath soft as a butterfly wing against her ear. The strands of her curly hair wrapped around his fingers, and he gave a small tug. "Look at me, Somiar. Feel...me."

She gazed into his hazel eyes, watching her own reflection in fascination. She knew what his body craved. He needed to feel her hands on him. She reached between their bodies and stroked his dick with long firm strokes. She stroked him faster and faster until his quaking body told her to stop. It was exciting to know she could anticipate his every desire, supply his every need. But it worked both ways.

He gently clasped her wrists and held them to her sides. His lips and tongue danced across her neck and moved lower, to draw one nipple into his mouth, then the other. She arched her back, not wanting the build-up of desire to stop. He kissed his way down her stomach, stopping to dip his tongue into her navel and work it in slow circles.

"Malachi." His name came out as a plea. He toyed with her and she loved it. It made her want him that much more.

His lips explored lower, tracing the joint of her thighs to

her pelvis, his tongue dragging along the crevice to the petal soft curls between her legs. Her body tensed in anticipation of what was to come. Her hips were held captive by his strong hands while his tongue barely touched the tip of her clit before he drew it into his mouth, gently sucking her. She shuddered, wanting so much for him to continue, but feeling like she would explode if he did. He slid two fingers deep inside her pussy, gliding them in and out, never releasing her from his mouth until Somiar came, convulsing and screaming his name.

Malachi slid his body up hers until they were face to face again. She teased his lips with her tongue, tasting herself on his mouth, her fingers grasping his ass. When Somiar drew her legs up to his waist he pushed them higher, over his shoulders and sank himself deep inside her. She gasped, not sure she would be able to accommodate him, but he moved slow and easy, taking her with him to the edge. He moved faster and faster, his muscles rippling under her hands. His breathing was deep and unsteady and his body quaked. The sound of her name on his lips as he came made her join him in climax.

He released her legs, but kept her close as he rolled to his side. "Even our hearts beat together."

She closed her eyes and felt their hearts pounding in unison. "Yes." And for the second time since this nightmare started, Somiar drifted off into a dreamless sleep.

Chapter 19

Malachi stood on the staircase in the gym beside Stephen watching as Somiar blocked Leila's punch and countered with a blow that Leila easily avoided. Even from this distance, the malice in Somiar's eyes was clearly visible. Ever since the night they'd encountered Monica, Somiar was like a different person. Besides taking up residence in his room and his bed, a change he loved, she immersed herself in the books they retrieved from Leila's grave.

Even though Somiar was a good fighter, she wasn't great. Stephen and Malachi took turns sparring with her and tutoring her in their specialties but Leila handled the majority of her training.

Lucien and Somiar were no longer allowed to spar each other. They went way beyond the boundaries of sibling rivalry. It was clear they resented one another and their last session had been brutal.. At one point, they had to be pulled apart. Stephen and Malachi did the majority of Lucien's training. Leila could hold her own when it came to fighting, so she sparred with him as well.

With a feral growl, Somiar swung at Leila. Leila ducked and grabbed Somiar by the arm, flipping her over her shoulder. Somiar landed on her back with a thud. Leila stretched one leg out over both of Somiar's thighs and drove a knee into Somiar's shoulder.

"Getting angry will get you killed." Leila stood, jerking Somiar up with her. "Control yourself."

Stephen frowned. "You think maybe we should stop this? They've been at it for over an hour and it's getting ugly."

"No. I think she needs to let off some steam. Leila won't hurt her. Teach her a lesson in self-control, maybe." Malachi took a long drink out of his water bottle. Truth be told, Somiar's viciousness worried him. She seemed mad at the world. She'd dropped him on his ass yesterday during weapons training. After disarming her, he retrieved her daggers and suggested they start again. Before he could finish talking, she kicked his legs out from under him then informed him that taking it easy on her would get her killed.

"Make no mistake, that girl is out for blood." Stephen slapped a hand on Malachi's shoulder and started up the stairs. "I'm glad I let you take the lead on this one, buddy. I hope you know what you're doing."

Malachi continued to watch the two women toss each other around like rag dolls. Unfortunately, Somiar hit the ground a lot more often than Leila.

"Enough!" Leila's voice echoed off the walls of the gym after slamming Somiar face down on the mat, pinning her in place. "I will not allow you to die because you insist on acting like a petulant child. If you'd let go of your anger, you might live long enough to hate me later."

Leila stalked to the stairs, pausing next to Malachi. "Talk to her. She's pissed, and I'm one of the people she's mad at. I can do nothing so long as she's like this. You should have let me get Monica that first night." She glanced back at Somiar, her eyes wistful. "Then all this would be behind us, and we could concentrate on our relationship."

He shook his head. "You can't guarantee you'll win against Monica. You owe Somiar a mother. I won't let you get out of paying your debt by dying before she's ready to let you go."

"Dying isn't in my immediate plans. But judging from the way she's been acting, I don't think she'd care one way or the other."

"She cares. She's just scared. Give her some time."

"I don't know how much time we have." Leila started up the stairs, her sweat soaked ponytail hanging limp down her back. "Got to heal some of these bruises and get back to my body. That girl packs quite a punch."

"I don't know if I'll ever get used to hearing that." Malachi descended the stairs and went to kneel beside Somiar. She had turned on her back and was staring at the ceiling. "Taking a nap?"

Without answering Somiar got up and wiped her hand on a towel.

Malachi tried to ignore the way her black sports bra hugged her breasts. Sweat trickled down her chest and disappeared beneath the fabric. Damp strands of brown hair had escaped the French braid and plastered themselves to the sides of her face. "What did you think you were doing just now? You were trying to hurt her."

When Somiar still didn't answer, Malachi grabbed her by her upper arm. "Hey, what's going on?"

"Hurt her?" Somiar yanked her arm from his grasp. "I'm the one who's been hurt. I was lied to about everything. I was lied to about who I am and what my purpose was, so forgive me if I'm just a little pissed about it."

"You know, playing the victim is really unattractive on you. Poor little Somiar, everyone has lied to here." Malachi didn't bother to hide the sarcasm in his voice. "Grow up. All of us have been lied to here. Lucien is in the same boat as you but he knows we have a job to do. Who do you think is upstairs guarding you and Leila right now?"

"I just wish I knew more about who I am. Learning it from a book isn't exactly cutting it." Somiar stared at her feet.

"You know exactly who you are. You're a good person with a good heart. A person who cares so much about family, you were willing to risk your life for a mother you knew nothing about. What you don't know about is your heritage. If you'd stop acting like a spoiled little brat, you'd have the opportunity to find out about that too. The answers to all of your questions is upstairs and you just tried to beat the crap out of her."

Malachi went back to the bottom of the stairs. "You coming?"

Somiar walked past, stopped two steps above him and turned. "Have I told you lately you're a pain in the ass when you're right?"

He pecked her lips. "No, but I like it that way."

"You like being a pain in the ass?"

"No, I like being right."

***

Somiar was ashamed of herself when she approached Leila. After training, she returned to her body and spent an hour trying to figure out how to apologize. "Can I talk to you out on the balcony?"

"Sure." Leila took her glass of water in hand. "Excuse me, gentlemen." Stephen, Malachi and Lucien nodded.

Somiar leaned against the waist high concrete wall surrounding the balcony and crossed her legs at the ankles. "I'm sorry about what happened in the gym. I don't know what's wrong with me. I shouldn't be taking my frustrations out on you. It's not you I'm mad at."

"Of course it is, and you have every right to be." Leila held up a hand when Somiar started to protest. "I left you with a lunatic, hid you from your father, and kept your whole history a secret. Granted, I was doing what I thought was best for you. But as they say, the road to hell is paved with good intentions." She took a sip from her glass. "I built a damned expressway."

For the first time, Somiar tried to see things from Leila's point of view. The last few days had taken its toll on her as well.

The past week had been a time for discovery. Time she used to find out about her culture and history. Through her great-grandmother's books, everyone had learned a little about themselves. Even Malachi and Stephen. After all, they all were part of the same culture. It wasn't a stretch to think that Leila was also discovering things on this journey.

Somiar sat beside to her on the chaise. "Don't worry. We'll work this out somehow." She chewed her lower lip, not sure if she wanted to bring back painful memories, but there were things she needed to know. "If I ask you an uncomfortable question, will you tell me the truth no matter how much you think it might hurt?"

The reservation in Leila's eyes was clear. "I'll try. What do you want to know?"

"Why didn't you come for me after Monica killed my father?"

"Believe me, had I known what she'd done, I would have killed her." Her eyes flashed and her lips thinned in a snarl. "I thought The Legacy had him killed because they found out about our relationship and about Lucien. My loving him was the ultimate betrayal in their eyes. Apparently, not many of us know the real deal about Dreamers and Catchers." She pressed her fingers to her temple. "I had no idea Monica was the Dreamer that got the job. As far as I knew, she had retired."

"Didn't the roses she kept in her study clue you in on who she was?" Somiar pacing the balcony, stopped dead in her tracks at Leila's confused expression.

"What are you talking about? What roses?"

"Monica's. She always kept a vase on her desk. The white vase full of black roses with one white rose in the center?" Somiar studied the blank look on Leila's face. How could she not know about Monica's roses? They'd been best friends. As well as they'd known each other, Leila had never been in Monica's study? "She didn't keep them when you were friends, did she?"

Before Leila could answer, the concrete wall next to her head splintered with a loud thwack. Small bits from the wall hit her in the temple abrading the skin.

Something whizzed past Somiar and shattered the glass

door behind her. She fell to her knees at the tug on her hand. Leila was on the ground pulling her down. "We need to get inside."

Malachi and Stephen flanked both sides of the door, guns drawn. She crawled with Leila across the balcony, trying to avoid glass fragments.

She was halfway through the door when Malachi grabbed her around her waist and quickly drew her in. Leila was right behind her. "Are you all right? Are you hurt?"

"No, I'm fine." Somiar allowed herself to collapse in Malachi's arms for a moment. "Thank God Monica's aim isn't what it used to be. I remember you said she never missed."

"Her record's still intact. I think she got who she was aiming for." Somiar followed Malachi's line of sight. Lucien was lying face down in front of the couch. He wasn't moving.

"Oh my God, is he okay?" Somiar tried to break free of Malachi's arms, but his grip on her tightened. "Wait."

Stephen pulled the cord next to the door, drawing the black curtains together. "Stay down."

"Lucien!" Leila crawled to Lucien and turned him over.

Lucien, covered in sweat, tried to crack a smile. "Damn, don't be so rough. I was just trying to heal this. It hurts like hell."

Leila examined the bleeding hole in his arm. "The bullet went straight through. You should be okay as long as we get some medical attention."

Somiar crawled over to sit next to them. "Malachi and Stephen have notified the Catchers about what's going on." She nodded towards Lucien's arm. "That's looks pretty bad."

"Why can't I heal this?" He struggled to a sitting position, ignoring Leila's protest, and leaned against the couch, sweat glistening on his face.

"Because you can't heal yourself. Haven't you read any of the books?" Somiar cocked her head to the side. Lucien seemed to be handling everything okay, but she just realized that he'd been avoiding her since their fight in the gym. Sure, he guarded her while her Dreamer body trained, but when she was awake, he made sure never to be alone with her. Had she not been so absorbed in her own misery, she would have realized he was hurting too.

Reaching out and taking his hand, she gave him a reassuring smile. "You should read them some time. She was your great-grandmother too. There are a lot of things in there about you."

"Yeah, like what?" Lucien swallowed and gazed at Somiar.

Malachi knelt next to him with an armful of bandages. He winked at Somiar and went to work on Lucien's arm.

"Well, we come from a long line of Dreamers and Catchers. There was a time when we lived in complete harmony with one another." She kept his hand in hers and sat against the couch next to him. "It was us against the world."

"Yeah?" He squeezed her hand and gave her an encouraging smile. "What else?"

"Well, if a Dreamer didn't have a mate, it was up to her father or brother to protect her while she protected her assignments. You're fantastic at your job little brother." She put her head on his shoulder. "We have a lot to learn about each other."

The double doors to the condo flung open. Three tall men in black jeans and t-shirts crossed the threshold. The one in the middle had long dreads twisted into a braid down his back. Both men on the end were identical and shaved bald. Red beams from their guns bounced off the furniture and walls.

"Any hearts still beating in here?" The middle man's voice was deep and strong.

"Get down," Malachi hissed. "She can't see us, but I don't think that'll stop her from shooting blind. Luke, we need you over here. Lucien's been hit. The bullet went straight through."

The man with the dreads came over to Lucien and checked his bandage. "Well, well. Welcome to the Catcher's Club, brother. You're now an official member." He tossed Leila a grin. "Nice to see you again. I think."

One of the bald men spoke up. "We're clear to go. Two Hummers at the private entrance. Four to a vehicle. You need to decide who rides with whom on the way down. No time for discussions. Let's move out."

The three newcomers headed out first, followed by the women, Stephen and Malachi supporting Lucien brought up the rear.

The group paused while Luke went outside to make sure the Hummers were secure. When he came back his expression was grim. "Both drivers are dead. There was a note attached to one of them." He stopped in front of Somiar. "It's for you."

Somiar took the note from him with shaking fingers. *"Come to me. You know how. It's in you. Come to me tonight, or they all die while you watch. One meeting with me and you'll never be this helpless again."* This was the last straw. Rage consumed her, and she ripped the note to shreds before they could take it from her. The line in the sand had been drawn. Monica had to be stopped.

Chapter 20

Somiar rested against Malachi's chest in the back of another Hummer procured from the Catchers. Luke didn't want to take the chance of using the ones they had. There was no way of telling what Monica had done to them. The twins, Enoch and Philip were up front. Somiar couldn't tell them apart and had no idea which one was driving. She was exhausted. The events of the day had finally taken their toll on her.

"Why did you tear up that note?" Malachi's rumbling voice was a comfort. It didn't matter that it was edged with a slight accusatory tone. She would have sounded the same way, had their positions been reversed. But, the sound of him, alive and well, was the encouragement she needed to face Monica.

"Please, Malachi. Why are you acting like you don't know what was in it?" She leaned back to study his face. "There's no way Luke gave me that note without reading it first." She narrowed her eyes. "And I know he told you what was there."

"Yes, he told me. My question is why didn't *you* tell me?"

Her face fell. "I don't know." Perhaps she didn't want to lose her mom. Maybe it was because she didn't want to lose a brother she didn't know she wanted. It could even be because she had a man by her side she could depend on. A man who could depend on her. A man she could love, and she didn't want to lose him either.

Love. There's a word that could get her nowhere fast. Her heart beat faster as the truth blindsided her. She did love him. And she knew she could trust him with her heart. But she also knew he would try to stop her from facing Monica, and that, she could not accept. Monica wanted her. And she would get her. Somiar rested her head back against his chest, and lied to him. Again. "I simply don't know."

***

Malachi pulled a black silk scarf from under the seat and held it up for Somiar to see. "I have to blindfold you." He and Stephen had agreed that Leila and Somiar didn't need to know how to get to the Keeper's headquarters.

"Okay." Her eyes glazed over and her lids fluttered. She closed her eyes, as if waiting for the silk to make contact with the delicate skin of her eyelids. Her breathing slowed, became deep and even.

"Somiar, wake up." Malachi gave her a gentle shake. "What's the matter with you?" When she didn't respond, his heart raced. "Baby, wake up. Come on, don't do this."

"Do what?" Her eyes opened a fraction. "Can we talk 'bout this in the morning? I'm tired."

"In the morning?" Malachi took a quick glance at his watch. "It's four in the afternoon. Did you take something? What did you take?" He lifted her lids and took a close look at her eyes. Her pupils were dilated. Not good.

"Something wrong, boss?" Enoch looked at him through the rear view mirror. "She okay?"

"I don't know. She keeps going out on me." He yanked his

phone out of his pocket to call the next car. Maybe they could shed some light on the situation. If someone drugged her, he would skin that someone alive.

Before he could dial the number, his phone buzzed. Stephen.

"Something's wrong with Somiar," he said before Stephen could speak. "I can't keep her awake and I don't remember her taking anything."

"We got a problem here too. Luke just fell asleep. We can't wake him up. The guy is snoring up a storm. He was definitely drugged."

Malachi could hear loud rumbling in the background. "How could anyone drug them? We were with them."

"You're not just anyone. You're Malachi." Somiar's slurred speech interrupted Malachi's response. "I love you." Her eyelids fluttered closed and her head lolled to the side. "You wouldn't do nothing to hurt me would you, Malachi?" She relaxed against him, knocked out. He lowered her head to his lap and tried to make sure she was comfortable.

Stephen chuckled. "Leila is wide awake and grudgingly serving as a pillow for Luke. He blindfolded her and then passed out. That just leaves one possibility. What was the one thing they both handled? The one thing that no one else came in contact with?"

Malachi's grip tightened on the phone. "The letter." He leaned his head back and sighed. "Who has the fragments?"

"Luke collected the pieces and put them back in his pocket. We'll get them tested and processed when we get to the lab, but I'm a hundred percent certain they're laced."

"Oh, this is bad. This is really bad. Rose is forcing Somiar to meet with her." Malachi stroked Somiar's hair back from her face. "And she may not come back."

Chapter 21

When the driver pulled into the Keeper's underground entrance and came to a stop, Malachi exited the black Hummer with Somiar in his arms.

Like the rest of the compound, the parking deck stark white, but years of exhaust fumes tinted the walls a dreary gray. Twelve multicolored Hummers lined the massive space, two spaces empty because of the trucks that were sent earlier in the day. According to Jared, they were cleared just minutes ago and en route. Thank God for his law enforcement connections. He wasn't the only Catcher on the force, but he was the most experienced.

Besides two mechanics and a few medical personnel, no one else was in the area. There was a gurney waiting to transport Lucien, and the attendants stated that two more were on the way for Luke and Somiar.

Malachi decided not to wait, and carried Somiar across the parking deck toward the elevators. There was no telling what was happening to her right now.

After Leila was led from her vehicle, she tore the blindfold from her eyes and ran toward them. "The guys said Lucien is going to be okay. They're moving him to the medical center for observation. They promised to let us know if there was any change in his condition." She brushed Somiar's hair back from her face. "Monica is going to pay for this."

"We have to get her in a room. Follow me." Malachi didn't wait for a response before he stepped onto the white elevator.

Leila jumped on with him. "I have to go in after her." She leaned against the wall and started planning. "When we get to a room, we'll get an IV started on me. It'll be the quickest route. I'm sure the letters were laced with Stardust."

"Stardust? What the hell is Stardust?"

"It's a synthetic sleeping agent the Legacy designed for Dreamers with insomnia." She gave a nervous chuckle at Malachi's expression. "Don't be so surprised. We're human. We're prone to the same problems as the rest of the world."

"Fine, but I'm going in too. She might need me." He couldn't take his eyes off Somiar. He needed a sign, any sign that she was okay. Right now, she was in a deep sleep. He just hoped her features would remain peaceful.

"No, Malachi. Thank you, but she's my child." Leila's voice was calm but firm. "I'll take care of her."

The muscle in his jaw twitched. "She stopped being your child a long time ago. If she needs me, I want to be there." The elevator doors opened. "I love her." Without another word, he stepped over the threshold and strode down the hall, Somiar held close in his arms.

***

"Dammit, I can't wake her." Malachi held smelling salts under Somiar's nose to no avail. In the back of his mind, there was a small glimmer of hope that he could wake her. In no way did he want her to have any contact with the Black Rose. She wasn't ready for that. Monica was the woman who raised her. He knew Somiar's emotions would get in the way. No way around it. He was not only frustrated, he was scared to death for her.

"Malachi, stop it." Leila grabbed his shoulders and pushed him away from Somiar. "That won't do any good. There's no waking her until that damn drug wears off. If Monica used Stardust on her, she could be out for hours. There's no antidote. That's why Dreamers only use it as a last resort." Leila looked him in the eye. "And I want to make one thing clear. Once we get dosed, game over. I don't want anyone waking us prematurely. We ride this out until the end." Leila yanked her sleeves up. "I'll have no problem tracking Somiar, but she has to pull you in."

"Let's go." Malachi pushed the buttons on his phone. "Stephen, give the letter to Enoch or Phil to take to the lab. Leila knows what it was laced with, but that's not important right now. We need you in the medical center. Suite five." After sticking his phone in his pocket, he sat on Somiar's bed and held her close. Her even breathing was reassuring to him. She was just sleeping. And for right now, hopefully, she was okay.

Leila put a strong hand on his shoulder. "Malachi, she can't beat Monica. Monica will destroy her."

"The hell she will. If she hurts a hair on Somiar's head, I'll kill her. I just hope Somiar can forgive me."

"She won't have too. Somiar can't beat her, but I can." Leila opened and shut the drawers on the red crash cart next to the hospital bed until she came across what she was looking for. After pulling several items out, she glanced up at Malachi. "You know how to start an IV?"

"Yeah. Lie back on the couch." When she was comfortable

on the plush blue couch at the end of Somiar's bed, Malachi tied the rubber tourniquet around her lower arm and slid the needle and catheter into a thick vein in her forearm. Next, he attached a bag of saline and pushed a small amount of amber fluid through one of her IV ports.

Stephen came bursting through the steel double doors of the suite. "What the hell do you think you're doing?"

Malachi drew up another dose for himself and signaled to Stephen. "Leila's going after Somiar, and I'm going too. There's a chance Somiar will pull me in but I have to be asleep." He looked over at Leila. "Can you still hear me.?"

Leila turned and gave him a sleepy, questioning glance. "Hmm?"

"If Monica hurts a hair on Somiar's head, she dies." He knelt next to her and looked into her eyes to make sure she was listening. "Do you understand me? She dies."

Leila gave him a thumb's up sign before her arm dropped to her side, and her breathing evened out.

Malachi stretched out next to Somiar and held his arm out for Stephen. "I don't have to have your help, but it would make things easier."

"I don't know about this Mal. It seems like a lot of crap to go through for a Dreamer." Stephen sat on a stool next to the bed.

"It could mean the end of the Black Rose, Stephen. We owe this to Richard. He didn't deserve what happened. Neither did Somiar, or Leila."

"I hope you know what you're doing, man." Stephen started Malachi's IV. "One sign that you're in danger, and I'm going to do what it takes to bring you back."

"The hell you will. I come out of this naturally." Malachi grimaced. "I know you're used to being the one to give the orders on this team, but just this once, let me see it through to the end."

Stephen picked up the pre-filled syringe from the bedside table and pushed it into Malachi's line. "If anyone can catch her, you can." He held is fist out to Malachi. "Not another Catcher dies on our watch."

Malachi tapped his fist against Stephen's. "Never again." He closed his eyes, keeping Somiar in his arms. "Bring it on, you crazy bitch."

Chapter 22

Somiar opened her eyes and tried to focus. The antique carousels from her childhood bedroom came into view. The last thing she remembered was talking to Malachi in the Hummer. Then... nothing. What the hell was going on? She hadn't intended to fall asleep. And why was she here?

The letter. Monica wanted to see her. And she had found a way to make sure she wasn't ignored. This is how it ends? Somiar took in her tight denim jeans, black tank top and frowned. This wasn't going to work. She closed her eyes and changed her clothes.

The comfortable orange silk pants and sleeveless shirt gave her freedom of movement and kept her cool. Silver handled daggers were sheathed and strapped to both thighs and arms. A pair of sai were sheathed and strapped across her back. Her hair was braided and pinned in a coil at the nape of her neck. Now she was ready to face off with Monica.

Somiar left her room and started her search of the house. Room by room she went, opening doors, her senses on high alert. There wasn't so much as a tingle along her spine to suggest Monica was in the house. She started to wonder if she just needed to rest and passed out in the Hummer. Her back against the wall, she closed her eyes and tried to will herself back into her body. Nothing. She was definitely drugged.

She descended the stairs, running her hand along the white wall, a habit that had annoyed Monica to no end when she was a child. Fingerprints on her mother's spotless walls had gotten Somiar grounded a countless number of times.

"Come out, come out wherever you are." she mumbled under her breath. "You want me, here I am." Opening the door to Monica's study, she stopped to survey the room. Nothing had changed here. Except the vase with the black roses. For as long as she could remember, that vase was always on the desk. Today, it was gone.

She opened the door to the game room, and there, on the pool table, was Monica's vase. It held four black roses and one white rose, each one with a tag hanging from it. Somiar went to the desk and lifted the tags on the black roses one by one. Leila. Lucien. Malachi. Somiar. And last she read the tag on the white rose. Somiar. Her name was on a black and white rose.

What the hell was that supposed to mean? The hairs on the back of her neck suddenly stood and her spine tingled. Monica was close. She could feel her. Her body came alive with raw, nervous energy. Somiar jumped back when the pool table started to slide back across the floor.

"Looking for me, Somiar?" Monica's sarcastic voice was unmistakable. It echoed off the walls of the room below.

Somiar descended the stone stairs to a part of the house she had never seen before. Monica stood at the bottom. The huge circular stone room was cold and uninviting. There were multiple monitors covering of one side of the room, emotionless female faces illuminating each screen.

"What's this?" Somiar took another glance around the

room before she turned to Monica. She was in her Dreamer body. The Black Rose, as Malachi had called her. Dressed in a black sleeveless leather cat suit, her hair hanging loose down her back.

"Aren't you one great big cliché?" Were her life not in danger, Somiar would have found the whole scene funny.

Monica scowled. "We're not here to talk about me. We're here to decide what to do about you." She indicated the screens with a sweep of her hand. "Somiar, I'd like you to meet the Legacy."

Somiar's mouth went dry, unable to tear her eyes from the beautiful women. "But you said no one meets the Legacy. You said you didn't even know who they were."

Monica shrugged. "I lied. Not only do I know who they are, I'm their leader." Monica prowled the room like a cat, finally stopping behind Somiar. "But I can't live forever." She placed her cold hands on Somiar's shoulders. "With your powers, you would be the prime candidate to take my place. You just have to do a couple of small things."

Somiar tried not to shrink back from Monica's touch. "And what would those small things be?"

"Let me kill Leila, and her abomination of a son. Your boyfriend will have to go too, but how well do you really know him anyway?" Monica had the same tone as someone who was chatting about the weather with a stranger.

It wasn't just Leila she was after. But Malachi and Lucien? It didn't add up. "I know why you want Leila gone. But why Lucien and Malachi?" Somiar turned to Monica and narrowed her eyes. "Lucien is a new Catcher, hardly a worthy opponent, and Malachi isn't any different from any other Catcher."

"Don't play dumb, Somiar." Monica snapped.

"What the hell are you talking about? Play dumb about what?"

"The Legacy knows about your great-great grandmother's diary. She was a Legacy member herself." Monica's lips twisted in a sneer.

Somiar shook her head. "No. That's not true. Leila would have told me..."

Monica rolled her eyes. "Why do you think Leila knows? Your great-great grandmother's Legacy name was Jasmine and I have her diary from her years as a Legacy member."

"Why would you have her diary?" Somiar wasn't sure she wanted to hear the answer. How long had the two families been at odds? If they went back that far, then Monica had to know who Leila's family was from the very beginning. It was probably why she befriended her.

"She and my grandmother served together. When the rest of the Legacy found out that Jasmine was trying to reunite the Dreamers and Catchers, they had to get rid of her." Monica advanced on Somiar, backing her against the wall. "But we found that Jasmine's journal during her years with The Legacy wasn't the only one. All Legacy members know the story of our heritage. The Legacy started the war. Think about it. Do you really want to share a culture with a bunch of women who need men to protect them? We've learned to take care of ourselves. We don't need protectors."

She planted her hands on the wall, pinning Somiar in

place. "We do what we want, when we want. To hell with the rest of the world."

Somiar couldn't believe her ears. All of this was over a diary? Monica and the Legacy had exterminated her family like cockroaches because of a book?

"Anyone with access to that diary is a threat to our way of life. We tried to get it from that damned Catcher years ago." Her face turned to a scowl. "But the damned fool forced me to kill him before I could get the location of the book." She walked away from Somiar with an agitated swagger to her stride.

Somiar glanced up at the faces on the screen. Their faces still filled the monitors, but they never said anything. Never showed any emotion. The only sign they were even conscious was a slight movement here and there.

It was time she did what she'd come to do. Somiar's fingers curled around the handle of the blade at her thigh. The Legacy never moved. She slid the knife halfway from its sheath. Nothing. Before she could fully release it, Monica whirled and threw her knife in Somiar's direction. It whizzed past her embedded itself in the wall right next to her head.

"Don't fuck with me, Somiar. I'm not in the mood." Monica strolled over and pulled her dagger from the wall, and returned it to the sheath on her arm. "Let's get down to business, shall we? The Legacy is here to bear witness to your decision. They will not interfere with anything that goes on here. Question of the day. Do you get a white rose, or a black one?" Her lips curved into a caustic smile. "We're even willing to forgive the fact that you're a freak of nature yourself. After all, you didn't get to pick your daddy."

The rage in Somiar's chest bubbled up to the surface. Before she could think about it, she balled her fist and punched Monica in the face with all her might.

Monica fell to the floor, blood spewing from her nose.

Funny. She didn't feel a thing as she watched Monica cover her nose, looking up at her in surprise. "Did you really think I would let you kill Leila?" Somiar circled Monica like a hawk stalking its prey, her breathing slow and even. Every cell in her body lusting for revenge. "Did you really think I would let you kill him?"

The depraved glint in Monica's eyes didn't faze her. It just made her blood thirsty. Monica was nothing more than a rabid animal that needed to be put down. Somiar would destroy her.

A short, evil laugh erupted from Monica's throat. "Let me? You really are full of yourself. I wasn't really asking for your permission. I was just being polite." As the blood from her nose faded from her face, she jumped to her feet. "You can't beat me, Somiar. You have two choices." She pulled two long sai from the sheaths strapped to her thighs. "Take your place with the Legacy, or die."

Somiar unsheathed her own sai and twirled the heavy metal in her hands enjoying the sound of the triple blades swishing in the air. "I'll take the third choice." She moved into fight position, legs wide, feet planted firmly to the floor. She raised one sai in front of her, the other over her head. "You die." Somiar advanced on Monica, swinging the blade over her head in an arc, aiming for Monica's neck. She thrust the weapon in her opposite hand toward Monica's chest.

Monica swung her blade up, blocking Somiar's descent

as she leaned back, her shoulders parallel to the floor. Silver sparks flew where their blades met. When she straightened, her arm swung in a graceful curve and the middle prong of her sai sliced into Somiar's hip.

Somiar cried out but resisted the urge to rub her injury and increased the speed of her thrusts, managing to cut into Monica's arm and cheek. Her blade scraped against bone, but the attacks were ineffective. Every time her sai cut into Monica's skin, the wound immediately healed.

Shit. Somiar hadn't learned to heal that fast. Her wounds were healing much slower than Monica's. Before the wound on her hip completely healed, Monica inflicted more cuts to her arms. Ignoring the blood and pain from the multiple flesh wounds on her arms, she continued to block and counter Monica's assault, looking for an opening where she could deliver a final lethal blow.

When Monica started to retreat from her thrusts, Somiar's confidence increased. If she could back Monica against the wall, she could defeat her. But, a few feet from her goal, Somiar detected the gleam of triumph in Monica's eyes.

In a lightning fast move, Monica turned and ran straight for the wall and up the side, flipping over Somiar's head, landing behind her. Before Somiar had a chance to turn, her feet left the floor, and she landed on her back. Her sai flew from both hands. It took a second for her to realize Monica had kicked her feet from under her.

Monica dropped on top of Somiar and drove a knee in her chest, limiting Somiar's breathing. "You fool. Would you really reject all that I have to offer?" Monica pulled an emerald and ruby handled dagger from its sheath at her arm and raised it high. Bringing it down in a swift arc, she ran the blade through Somiar's hand, embedding the tip in the rough wooden floor below.

Somiar screamed in pain. Her head spun as she watched the blood seep from the wound onto the old wood floor. So long as the blade remained in her hand, she couldn't heal. And Monica knew that.

"All the power of the Legacy could be yours. You'll have total control of the Dreamers, and because of what you can do, the Catchers as well. They'll be at your mercy." Monica pulled another dagger from its sheath. "I can teach you how to wield that power. Surrender the life of the woman who abandoned you, and the lives of two men who think you're trash."

Somiar stared long and hard in Monica's eyes. She could have sworn she saw a flash of pain.

Monica winced and put a hand to her head. Then the cold evil glint returned. "Which is it Somiar? Do you join us or do you die?"

Somiar raised her head and spit in Monica's face. "Go to hell."

"Wrong answer." Monica drove the dagger into to Somiar's other hand burying it in the wood floor to the hilt.

The pain was unbearable. Somiar screamed until her throat was raw, sweat and tears running down her face. Both hands pinned to the floor, and fighting to stay conscious, Somiar tried to take in gulps of air, but Monica pressed her knee harder against her chest.

"It doesn't have to end this way," she said. "The Legacy is your birthright. Don't make me kill you." Monica's voice was cold with a hint of desperation. "I'm running out of time."

Somiar didn't know what that was supposed to mean.

"Monica, you coward."

The words barely registered in her pain ridden mind. Where had they come from?

"Why don't you face the one you really want? This is our fight."

Leila! Could it be? Somiar prayed that her mother's voice wasn't a figment of her imagination.

Monica's lips spread into a slow smile. Blood lust and rage filled in her eyes. "It looks like the choice is no longer yours, my dear."

Somiar watched in horror as Monica rose and ran toward Leila, her sai poised and ready for battle. The room started to tilt. She had trouble keeping her eyes focused. The sounds of metal crashing against metal invaded her brain. Everything was louder than it should have been. She knew she was losing a lot of blood, but she had to get away. There was only one hand she had a chance of freeing. Holding her breath, she yanked her hand up the blade to the hilt. Warm blood ran down her arm from the widened wound. With all the strength she could muster, she took a deep breath and jerked her palm up against the jeweled handle freeing the tip from the floor. Taking great gulps of air, she tried to breathe through the pain. Don't scream. Everything was going hazy. Malachi! His name rang out like a roar in her head. Then, her world went black.

Chapter 23

Malachi opened his eyes and tried to focus. At first, all he could make out was a gray stone ceiling. The deafening sound of metal clanging metal registered in his muddled mind. Rubbing his eyes, he sat up and gasped at the sight in front of him. Monica and Leila were going at each other like wild women. They both wielded a long black sai in each hand and doing some heavy-duty fighting. Leila had resumed the dreamer body she'd used the first night he saw her at Lucien's party. Her black braid whirled around her as she blocked and countered every thrust Monica threw her way.

Behind them was a wall of monitors, the beautiful faces on them passively watching the fight. One of the faces turned her attention to him and her screen went blank. One by one the women noticed him and disconnected.

"Looks like your friends have deserted you," Leila taunted. When Monica glanced at the screens, Leila crossed her sai out in front of her, latched one of Monica's and knocked it from her hand.

Monica lunged at Leila with the other sai. When Leila ducked, Monica shot out a leg and kicked Leila square in the chin, knocking her backward toward the stairs.

Leila tried to break her fall but hit her head on the bottom step. She landed in a crumpled heap, blood seeping from her temple.

Monica stalked over to where Somiar lay and slapped her soundly across the face. "What did you do, you little bitch? Why did the Legacy leave?"

With his path cleared, Malachi lunged for Leila to help her, but then saw Monica standing over Somiar. Until that moment, he hasn't seen her lying there. Monica was backing away from Somiar, her expression horrified.

He sprinted across the room and grabbed Monica around the throat. "What have you done!" He flung her from him as if she weighed no more than a pound. Her body crashing against the wall.

Blood poured from the gaping hole in Somiar's free hand. He pulled off his shirt before withdrawing the blade from her palm. When the bleeding increased, he wrapped his shirt around her hand hoping to stop the flow.

He didn't want to yank the knife from her pinned hand. It would cause more profuse bleeding. For some reason, she wasn't healing. "Somiar. Wake up, Somiar! You've got to heal yourself." Malachi gently took her chin in his fingers and turned her head toward him. He almost fell backwards when he saw her face. Her eyes were completely white.

"Malachi? Is that you? I can't see." Somiar's voice came out in a shaking whisper.

"Oh my God what did they do?" He turned to where Monica was crouched on the floor, her hands pressed to her temples. "He stalked over to her, his mouth a rigid line, hand balled into fists at his sides. "What did you do?"

When she didn't answer, he bent over her and seized a handful of her hair. "What did you do to her?" he shouted.

Monica cut her eyes at him. "I did nothing. Her death will be on your head. I offered her a family, sisterhood, the world. You can offer her nothing.

Before Malachi could blink, she sank her teeth deep in his arm, drawing blood. His grasp on her loosened, she wrenched away, grabbed a discarded knife from the floor and held the point over his heart.

His blood coated her bared teeth, but she didn't seem to notice. "Before I kill you just remember this one thing. She is going to die, and so will her abomination of a brother."

"Go to hell, bitch." Leila's voice barely had time to register before the tip of a sai pushed its way through Monica's chest. Leila twisted the blade before snatching it out. Blood spurted Malachi's chest and arms, and gushed down Monica's torso, pooling at her feet.

Malachi pushed Monica away, knocking her on her back before she could fall on top of him. The blood pool under her continued to spread.

She gurgled and coughed, sending more blood flying. Then, silence. Her empty eyes stared up at Malachi like a lifeless curse.

Leila stood glaring at Monica's dead body, the prongs of her sai dripping with Monica's blood.

"There's something wrong with Somiar." Malachi wrenched the weapon from Leila's hand and tossed it aside. "She's blind and can't heal." Malachi ran back to Somiar's side, Leila hot on his trail. "What's wrong with her?"

"I don't know. I've never seen this before." Leila brushed

stray strands of hair from Somiar's face. "Come on baby, you've got to heal this. Heal your hand, so we know it safe to free the other one." Tears rushed from Leila's eyes. "Please, Somiar."

"I can't. I'm trying, but I don't know what's wrong." Somiar sobbed hysterically. Her chest heaved as she took in great gulps of air. "Why can't I see?"

Footsteps pounded down the stone stairs and about a dozen Catchers flooded the room. Their rings glowed when they came close to Leila. Two Catcher's grabbed her arms and wrenched them behind her back. A third pointed a gun at her head.

Somiar eyes suddenly returned to normal, and the wound to her hand started to heal. Malachi didn't know why it happened nor did he care. He bent over her, his hand on the knife in her impaled hand. "Sweetheart, listen to me. I have to take this out okay? It's going to hurt like hell but it'll only last a minute."

Somiar nodded, her eyes full of trust.

He clutched the handle with both hands and pulled, surprised at how deep it was buried in the wood. The muscles in his arm flexed and bulged as he withdrew the knife as fast as he could.

Somiar's ear-splitting scream echoed off the walls. She sobbed and shivered uncontrollably.

He took her in his arms and held her tight. "Okay, baby. Heal yourself." He ran his hand up and down her sweat soaked back. When she quieted, he drew away and studied her hands. There wasn't a mark on them. He put a hand to her cheek. "You okay?"

Somiar leaned forward and kissed him passionately. "Better than okay." She buried her face in his shirt. "Where's Monica?"

"She won't hurt you again." When Somiar tried to turn, he held her in place. "Don't. You don't need to see that." Malachi looked up at the Catcher's from his position on the floor. "What's going on? How'd you guys get here?"

"Um, Malachi, a little help here?" Leila was less than happy at being manhandled.

"It's all right guys. Believe it or not, she's on our side. How'd you know we were here?"

Jared stepped forward. "Stephen gave us a heads-up. Apparently, our newbie can do some things the rest of us can't." He nodded at Somiar. "Lucien was able to see everything that went on here, through her eyes."

"Oh really?" Malachi gave Leila a scathing look. "I'm sure there's a good reason you left out the fact he could do that?"

"Don't give me that look. I had no idea." Leila rolled her eyes heavenward. "I'm sure there's a reason Grandma didn't mention it in her diary."

Somiar pulled back from Malachi. "Maybe she didn't know. Maybe we evolved somehow. Anyway, I'd rather Lucien not do that in the future without warning. Apparently, when he looks through my eyes, I can't see or heal. I don't like being blind." She stared down at her hands. "And I definitely don't like not being able to heal."

Another Catcher stooped with what looked like a remote control poised over Monica. "We got a lock on her body." He pounded at the keys on his device, pulled a dreamer pin from a case, and rammed it in Monica's lifeless neck.

Somiar couldn't help but to look over to where Monica's

body lay and shivered. She quickly returned her face to the warmth of Malachi's chest.

Malachi encircled Somiar in a protective embrace. "Where is she?"

"Piedmont Hospital." Jared stepped back as Monica's body started to fade. The blood on the wall and floor disappeared, as well as Monica's blood on Malachi and Leila's sai.

Somiar turned and stared as all traces of Monica dying there, disappeared. "What the hell is she doing in Piedmont Hospital?"

Jared eyed Somiar as if she was crazy. "Been there in a coma for the past two days. She has a brain tumor." He raised a brow. "She didn't tell you she was dying?"

It was then Somiar remembered something Monica said during their fight. *I don't have much time.* "No. She didn't."

"Damn, that's some cold shit. Luke found out about the brain tumor a couple of hours ago. He had one of our hackers break into her medical records, which was no easy feat. They were pretty heavily encrypted. And we had one hell of a time tracking her down. She was found unconscious in a hotel in Catalonia. She had checked in under an assumed name. They had no way of identifying her." Jared surveyed the room. "Her papers were located, and she was flown back here. According to the hospital, Miss Ayers, they were trying to reach you."

"They couldn't reach me because someone," she cast a side-long glance at Malachi, "destroyed my phone."

Malachi looked sheepish. "Hey, I didn't know she could track you."

Jared squatted next to Leila's sai and inspected it, looking for any trace of Monica's blood. "Just as well. It'll give us the perfect cover story about her death. A woman with that much money can't just up and croak of a mysterious illness."

At Somiar's distressed look, Malachi cleared his throat loudly. "Can it, Jared."

Jared flushed. "I'm sorry Miss Ayers. I wasn't thinking." At Somiar's slight nod he jerked a thumb at the monitor covered wall. "What's with all the monitors?"

Somiar could feel the color drain from her face. She tried to keep her voice from shaking. "The faces on the monitors. They were all Legacy members and Monica said she was the leader."

"Dammit!" Jared threw up his hands. "You mean we just let the head of the Legacy slip through our fingers? Capturing her alive could have meant an end to the Dreamers."

Leila, hands on her hips, glared at Jared. "When this is over, remind me to give you a little history lesson. You're going to be surprised at what comes falling out of your family tree."

"Yeah, yeah." He waved a dismissive hand at Leila. "Maybe we can get the information we need from the hard drive." Jared looked at the monitors. "Yo, Noah!"

The tall, husky man that pinned Monica rushed over. "What do you need?"

"Select a detail and get this terminal back to headquarters. Just be careful. I don't want anything damaged." He rubbed his hands together. "This could be the answer to our prayers."

The sound of footsteps pounding down the stairs made everyone turn. Stephen bounded into the room, gun drawn, looking for a fight. "Damn! Did I miss all the action?"

Everyone laughed at Stephen's crestfallen look. He sauntered over to Malachi and Somiar, and stooped down beside them. "Glad you're still alive." After motioning Leila over to join them, he held out his fist. "Not another Catcher," he looked at both ladies, "or Dreamer dies on our watch. At least, not without knowing the truth." They all tapped their fists together. He pulled out his phone. "What do you say I get the doctor to wake you guys up?"

Malachi was about to agree when Leila stopped him. "Not so fast Mal. We have to wait until the Stardust wears off. There's no antidote. You don't want to leave Somiar alone, do you?" She brushed the escaped tendrils from her braid out of her eyes. "I'll go back. You stay with Somiar. I'll make sure nobody wakes you until she comes out of it. Besides, I want to check on Lucien."

Stephen returned the phone to its case. "Fine. I'll go help the team with the cleanup and a cover story for what went on here today. A few nosy neighbors may have to have their memories erased." He followed several catchers back upstairs. Three men remained behind and began taking apart the computer terminal.

"Hmm. I wonder what we can do until I wake up?" Somiar gave Malachi a devilish smile. "Want to go back to Jamaica?"

He threw his head back and laughed. "I think I can get used to being married to a Dreamer."

Somiar and Leila froze. "Married?" They spoke in unison.

Everyone in the room stopped what they were doing to look at him. For the first time in his life, he felt self-conscious. His heart sank to his feet. The last thing he wanted to do was freak Somiar out. He didn't know why he said what he did. The words rolled off his tongue as naturally as his own name.

They belonged together. He'd never been more sure of anything in his life. "If you'll have me."

"If you don't say yes, I have a fool for a daughter."

"I'm going to say yes, Leila. I love him," Somiar smiled. "I can't think of anything I want more."

Leila quirked a brow. "Um, I didn't say anything. Out loud." She narrowed her eyes and took a step toward Somiar. *"Can you hear me?"*

"Of course I can hear you, but why aren't your lips..." her words trailed off into a whisper, "moving?" She lightly rubbed her temples trying to make sense of what was happening. "The night you were captured. I could hear your voice. You wanted to know why I wasn't wearing the necklace."

Leila had to remind herself to close her mouth. "You heard me?"

"Yeah, I could hear you. But the next time we were together, I couldn't. It must only work if both of us are dreaming."

Malachi cleared his throat. "Seems like we all have a lot of learning to do." He drew Somiar close and looked deep into her eyes. "But right now, I'm more interested in us."

Somiar pulled his head toward her for a kiss. Then she started laughing. Hard.

He pulled back and quirked a brow. "You know, one of these days you're going give me a big case of performance anxiety. First, you push me off a cliff after we make love, and now you laugh after I kiss you. What gives?"

Trying to suppress a giggle, Somiar smiled. "I just thought about my name after I marry you. Somiar Walker. Translation, please?"

"Dream Walker." Joining in her laughter, he hopped to his feet and held out a hand to help her up.

Somiar smiled and gracefully rose to her feet without his help. "See, fit as a fiddle." She stood on her toes and kissed his chin. "Now what about that trip to Jamaica?"

"Excuse me you two." Leila waved her hand at them. "None of us are going anywhere if we don't get out of this crowd." With a mischievous smile, she leaned in so only Somiar and Malachi could hear. "If you want to really freak them out, tell them to turn their backs."

Malachi returned her grin. He looked from Leila to Somiar. "You guys ready to zap out of here?"

Chapter 24

The hot summer air smelled of fresh cut grass. A gentle breeze weaved its way through the leaves and blooms of massive trees. There was no sound, save the pastor reading scripture from a worn bible.

Somiar sat in front of the flower laden, mahogany casket that housed Monica's body. Although Monica had turned out to be a monster, Somiar couldn't help but shed a few tears. Her tears weren't so much for losing the woman everyone thought was her mother. She mourned growing up, never knowing a mother's love. Malachi stood behind her, hands resting lightly on her shoulders. She reached up to clutch one of them taking comfort in the reassuring squeeze of his fingers.

Lucien and Stephen kept watch in the crowd of guests, in case any of the Legacy would dare show their faces. Of course, it would be foolish of them to show up here, in their Dreamer bodies, but life proved to be full of surprises.

The guests filed by, taking a flower from the top of the coffin and headed for their cars. Somiar stood, but didn't leave the spot. Instead, she stared, almost forgetting to breathe, as the casket was lowered into the cement lined earth.

"You don't have to watch this, sweetheart," Malachi's deep

voiced rumbled. He wrapped his arms around her and inhaled the pomegranate scent of her hair.

"She's really gone," Somiar's voice broke on the last sentence. She turned to bury her face in Malachi's black shirt. "The woman who raised me is dead, and left me a lifetime of looking over my shoulder, waiting for the next loon to come after me." She turned to Lucien, who had come to stand next to her. "After us." Her musings were interrupted when 'Wild Thing' blared from Stephens phone.

With a sheepish look, he drew his phone from his pocket. "What's up Lee?" He stepped away from the group to continue his conversation with Leila.

Somiar and Lucien exchanged knowing looks. They all knew Stephen and Leila had the hots for each other, why they kept playing coy was anyone's guess. They could both go from zero to fifty in a split-second when it came to making a point.

She remembered the shouting match they had when discussing Monica's funeral. Stephen threatened to pin her if she came anywhere near the funeral today. Especially since she was the one who killed her. His stance was reinforced when she declared the only reason she wanted to be there was to spit on 'the bitch's' grave.

"Those two should just get down and dirty and get it over with," Malachi mumbled.

Before Somiar could answer, a familiar chill raced from the top of her neck to her tailbone. She glanced around, half expecting the Legacy to attack. "Um, dear. I think we've got company."

Malachi scanned the cemetery, but could see nothing unusual. None of their rings glowed. A few male reporters hovered, but kept their distance. Monica was a high-profile society celeb in Atlanta and Malachi made sure they didn't make a nuisance of themselves so Somiar could handle her feelings her way, in her own time. "You sure?"

"She's right, Mal. My ears are ringing like crazy." Lucien's gaze surveyed the area, trying to spot anything out of the ordinary.

As Stephen walked past a group of reporters and news crew, his irritation with Leila plain on his face, the eerie red light blazed from his right hand.

"Die, Catcher!" One of the news crewmen drew a dagger from behind the camera and sent it twirling toward Stephen.

The knife grazed his cheek, deep enough for the area to bleed profusely. Stephen dropped to his knees, blood pouring between his fingers, his phone falling next to him in the grass.

As the rest of the crew and reporters scattered for cover behind crypts and tombstones, the one who threw the knife sprinted toward the rear of the mausoleum.

Malachi shouted to Lucien and Somiar, "Help Stephen," then ran top speed after the cameraman.

Stephen, holding his handkerchief to his face, stared at the mausoleum, eyes wide. "It can't be!"

"Don't talk, Stephen. That's making it worse." Somiar glanced past Stephen, looking for any sign of Malachi.

Lucien jerked his jacket from his back, then yanked his white shirt off to add pressure to Stephen's cheek.

Somiar placed her hand over his. "You can heal him, Lucien. Remember what Leila taught you."

"Hello! What the hell is going on? Stephen, are you okay?

Answer me!" Leila's voice screeched through the phone that was still laying in the grass.

Somiar picked up the phone, trying to assist Lucien and Stephen while balancing the cell phone in her lap. "Leila, don't panic. There's a Dreamer here, but we can't find her. I could sense her, and Stephen's ring detected her, but there are no women in close proximity. The Legacy may have hired a hit from an outside source."

"Is Stephen okay? I want to speak to him. Put him on the phone!" Leila yelled.

"Listen Leila, now is not the time to..."

Before Somiar could finish, Stephen took the phone from her, his cheek showing no signs of his injury. "I'm okay, Lee. Calm down."

"Don't tell me to calm down. Someone just tried to kill you! Where are my children?" Leila was loud enough for all of them to hear her.

Malachi jogged over to the group. "Okay, ya'll aren't going to believe this shit."

Somiar looked up. "You couldn't catch him?"

Malachi shook his head. "I found the real camera man knocked out behind the mausoleum, gagged and hogtied. The Legacy has never hired someone for a hit before. Whoever that guy was, he's good at covering his tracks. Good thing his aim sucks."

"I think he did what he was sent to do." Somiar nibbled her lip. "He was a warning."

Lucien helped Stephen to his feet. "We're going to need some damage control," he inclined his head in the direction of several people hiding, cell phones and cameras pointed in their direction.

"It's handled." Malachi inclined his head toward several unmarked cars pulling alongside the path to Monica's grave. "We kept Jared and his crew on standby just in case the Legacy showed up. No one will remember this. All the people close enough to see what actually happened will have their memory wiped. All cameras will show someone attempt to take out Somiar's bodyguard."

"Oh, that's rich," Stephen mumbled. "Now I'm her bodyguard."

"We need to get out of here before this gets really ugly," said Malachi. "Let the Keepers do their jobs."

Somiar put a shaking hand on Malachi's arm. "What everyone else saw is the least of our worries.

The three men turned to her, but only Malachi spoke. "What?"

"Let's go home." Somiar didn't wait for a response before heading toward the car.

***

Somiar crossed the room of Malachi's penthouse and poured herself a cognac. After several seconds, she decided to pour one for Malachi, Lucien and Stephen. She handed them their glasses. "I'm afraid we're in big trouble."

Stephen rolled his eyes at the rapid pounding on the front door. "I'd recognize that insufferable noise anywhere." The fact that he knew who it was didn't keep him from glancing at the camera monitor before opening the door.

Leila stomped over the threshold without invitation. "Anyone want to start explaining that commotion in the cemetery?" She gave Stephen the side-eye. "And I can't be responsible for what I'll do if I find either one of you put my children in danger."

Somiar wasn't in the mood for Leila's crap. She wanted so hard to remind her mother that she was the reason they were in this predicament. Had she not lied about Lucien's and Somiar's parentage, and had the guts to stand up to the Legacy, things could have been a lot different. Of course, life wouldn't have been easy, but everything would be out in the open, and they all could have started searching out Dreamers and Catchers and spreading the truth of their origins. "I think everyone should sit and take a sip, because what I'm about to tell you is going to be a game changer."

No one spoke. Somiar leveled her gaze to Malachi. "The man you were chasing is a Dreamer."

"That's impossible!" Leila jumped to her feet. "Dreamers are women."

"How do you know their actual bodies don't belong to women?' Somiar turned to Leila.

"We can't switch genders," Leila said.

Leila turned to Malachi. "Did the cameraman you were chasing look like the real cameraman?"

"No. The commentator was told he was a replacement because their regular person was sick. They were so pressed for time to cover the funeral, no one had time to verify his story." He ran a hand across his head. "The Dreamer was probably in disguise."

"Well, I got to see him up close and personal, and that didn't look like a disguise," Stephen interjected. "And he definitely had a man's voice."

"You think the Legacy has found a way to change genders?" Leila slid her hands in the back pockets of her jeans.

"Well, Lucien and I can sense a Dreamer faster than any of you, thanks to our mixed blood. And we're sure the cameraman was a Dreamer."

Lucien downed the rest of his drink. "I guess the Legacy did find a way to attend the funeral. Imagine the damage they could do if they passed how to do this to the Dreamers loyal to them. They're way ahead of us."

Everyone fell silent as they contemplated his words. What he proposed was very possible. What one member knew, they all knew. The legends were passed throughout the generations. Problem was, the less convenient parts were left out. Thanks to the Legacy, the Dreamers didn't know they were fighting and unnecessary war.

Somiar addressed the group. "We need to stick together."

Malachi stood and hugged her around the waist. "We're also going to have to learn to trust each other."

The rest of their group stood and joined in a circle. All of them could feel the connection. Each to the other. The way it was meant to be.

Chapter 25

Eighteen months later

Somiar lay on the table trying to ignore the thick, cold goop on her stomach for her ultrasound.

Malachi concentrated on the monitor, squinting as if that would make the image on the screen any clearer.

The doctor rolled the wand over Somiar's protruding abdomen, trying to get the best picture, and chuckled. "Well. It seems there's no reason to worry over your weight gain, Mrs. Walker. Would you two like to know the sex of your babies?"

Malachi and Somiar looked at each other in astonishment. "Babies?" they both asked in unison.

"Yes, babies. Three. Would you like to know the sex?"

"Three?" Malachi paled. "Did you say three?"

Somiar gave his hand a reassuring squeeze. She had the same questions he did. Were they having Dreamers or Catchers? "We want to know."

"Well, so far, we have a boy and a girl. As for the other one, that part is out of view."

"It's a boy." Malachi squeezed Somiar's hand. "I've seen him. I've seen them all. They're beautiful, perfect babies."

Somiar gave a little laugh. "Malachi. Every man wants a son, two sons I'm sure are a blessing. I just don't want you to be disappointed if he turns out to be she."

He leaned in close and looked into her eyes. "You don't understand. I've seen them. Really seen them. The night I bought you to the condo. Remember, it's a perk of being a Catcher." He held her close, like he never wanted to let her go. "They've been in my heart since before they were conceived."

Somiar stroked his face and let her joyful tears flow. "Three babies. We never do anything half-way do we?"

Malachi smiled down at her. "I guess not. I knew life with you would never be dull."

The End